"You know that t
about that never l

D0328625

"For the record, you c
on that table over ther
out of it, but that won't change anything. The fact is that we did it."

"You're not wrong about that." She looked everywhere but at Leo.

This was really starting to get on his nerves. "What's going on, Tess? Just spit it out."

"I'm pregnant."

He blinked at her and couldn't wrap his mind around the words. "I'm sorry. What?"

"I'm going to have a baby."

Bingo. That was the scariest thing she could have said to him. He couldn't believe it. No way this was happening to him. Not again.

Dear Reader,

When you meet someone for the first time, do you look for a "click"? The gut feeling that this person could be a best friend forever? They'll get your wacky sense of humor and know what you're thinking even before the thought pops into your mind. I have experienced that and it's pretty great when it happens. But sometimes a relationship grows in spite of a bad first impression.

In *An Unexpected Partnership*, Tess Morrow's reaction is the opposite of a "click" when she meets Leo "The Wall" Wallace. She takes an instant dislike to the cocky, ex–hockey player turned entrepreneur who wants to buy into her family's business. But on the night of her grandfather's memorial service, Leo's comforting gesture turns into white-hot passion. A few weeks later Tess finds herself in the family way and on the brink of financial ruin, in danger of losing everything her grandfather worked for and spent his life building. The last thing she wants is to tell Leo he's going to be a father. Oh, and by the way, could you partner up with me after all and save my business?

Leo has deeply painful reasons for not believing the cool-as-ice woman who melted in his arms. But as long as there's any chance the baby is his, he's going to stick around if it kills him. And fighting his growing feelings for the sexy businesswoman just might.

It was such fun writing Tess and Leo's dialogue! I hope you enjoy their story and the spirited interaction between these two strong-willed people as much as I loved writing it.

Happy reading!

Teresa Southwick

An Unexpected Partnership

Teresa Southwick

If you purchased this book without a cover you should be aware that this book is stolen property. It was reported as "unsold and destroyed" to the publisher, and neither the author nor the publisher has received any payment for this "stripped book."

Recycling programs for this product may not exist in your area.

ISBN-13: 978-1-335-57379-7

An Unexpected Partnership

Copyright © 2019 by Teresa Southwick

All rights reserved. Except for use in any review, the reproduction or utilization of this work in whole or in part in any form by any electronic, mechanical or other means, now known or hereafter invented, including xerography, photocopying and recording, or in any information storage or retrieval system, is forbidden without the written permission of the publisher, Harlequin Enterprises Limited, 22 Adelaide St. West, 40th Floor, Toronto, Ontario M5H 4E3, Canada.

This is a work of fiction. Names, characters, places and incidents are either the product of the author's imagination or are used fictitiously, and any resemblance to actual persons, living or dead, business establishments, events or locales is entirely coincidental.

This edition published by arrangement with Harlequin Books S.A.

For questions and comments about the quality of this book, please contact us at CustomerService@Harlequin.com.

® and TM are trademarks of Harlequin Enterprises Limited or its corporate affiliates. Trademarks indicated with ® are registered in the United States Patent and Trademark Office, the Canadian Intellectual Property Office and in other countries.

Printed in U.S.A.

HARLEQUIN®
www.Harlequin.com

Teresa Southwick lives with her husband in Las Vegas, the city that reinvents itself every day. An avid fan of romance novels, she is delighted to be living out her dream of writing for Harlequin.

Books by Teresa Southwick

Harlequin Special Edition

The Bachelors of Blackwater Lake

Finding Family...and Forever?
One Night with the Boss
The Rancher Who Took Her In
A Decent Proposal
The Widow's Bachelor Bargain
How to Land Her Lawman
A Word with the Bachelor
Just a Little Bit Married
The New Guy in Town
His by Christmas
Just What the Cowboy Needed

Montana Mavericks: The Lonelyhearts Ranch

Unmasking the Maverick

Montana Mavericks: The Baby Bonanza

Her Maverick M.D.

Montana Mavericks: What Happened at the Wedding?

An Officer and a Maverick

Montana Mavericks: 20 Years in the Saddle!

From Maverick to Daddy

Mercy Medical Montana

Her McKnight in Shining Armor
The Doctor's Dating Bargain

Visit the Author Profile page
at Harlequin.com for more titles.

To my friend Vicki Kahler Goeres. It seems like yesterday we were new neighbors who clicked immediately and bonded over our hair. We don't live on the same street anymore, but the friendship is still going strong. Thanks, buddy.

Chapter One

Tess Morrow needed to cry.

Grief had been trapped in her chest all day, and the pressure to let it go grew more painful by the second. She'd been strong during her grandfather's memorial service here at The Pub. All Patrick Morrow's friends had shared their stories of him, the funny, generous, kind man who'd raised her, and she hadn't shed a tear. People offered condolences and she gracefully thanked them. But if one more person said "I'm sorry for your loss," the composure that was making her face hurt would shatter. If the stragglers didn't leave pretty soon, she couldn't guarantee they wouldn't see her ugly, wet, snotty cry.

She both yearned and dreaded to be alone when it happened. Still, the sooner she sped up them up, the sooner she could mourn privately.

She walked over to the booth by the front window and smiled at the three men and one woman there. They were here to pay their respects. "Can I get you anything? Another beer? Glass of wine?"

All four shook their heads. They were older, longtime friends of her grandfather. Silver-haired John Alexander gave her a sympathetic look. "How are you holding up, honey?"

"Okay," she lied. "I learned how to be strong from him."

"That was Pat," he agreed. "Strongest person I ever knew."

The older woman sitting beside him touched his arm and gave the other two men a look. "We need to go. It's been a long day for Tess."

The others murmured their agreement and slid out of the booth. Every one of them asked if she needed anything and then hugged her. Made sure she knew to call if they could help her at all. Finally, blessedly, she closed and locked the door behind them. She lowered the shades on the big glass windows looking out on the nearly empty parking lot. Finally she was alone.

"Tess?"

She whirled around, heart pounding. "Dear God, Leo. You scared the crap out of me."

"Sorry. I didn't mean to."

"What are you doing here?" She blew out a long breath.

"I came to pay my respects to Pat," he said. "He was my friend."

"I meant *still*. What are you still doing here?"

"Just wanted to stick around. Make sure you're okay." He shrugged one broad shoulder.

Leo "The Wall" Wallace used to play professional ice hockey up until two years ago when an ankle injury ended his career. That sucked for him, but prevented female heartbreak in every major city with an NHL team.

He was a really big man, not just tall, but muscular, too. He had dirty-blond hair that insisted on curling and blue eyes that normally sparkled with mischief and flirtation. Right now they were somber and a little sad. Her grandfather had had a soft spot in his heart for this man. Tess's heart? Not so soft for him.

"Where did you come from?" Her pulse was finally slowing to normal.

"My favorite booth."

She glanced at it in a far, shadowy corner that Pat had

called the penalty box. In honor of Leo and his time spent in one during his hockey career.

"Well, I didn't see you." That was only half a lie. She'd ignored him, or tried to. He was a reminder of problems—personal and otherwise.

In the last year or so, bar revenue had declined. They were losing business to trendier establishments, and six months ago her grandfather had approached Leo about investing in The Pub. He'd introduced her and suggested lending Leo's celebrity name and a bit of capital to modernize and shake things up. She'd assured Pat that the two of them together could come up with a plan to make the place profitable again. But he was sick. Losing the man who'd taken her in when she was six years old hadn't been part of that plan.

Tears stung her eyes but she managed, just barely, to hold them back. "I'm fine."

He moved closer, stopping right in front of her. The man was like a mountain. Hence his nickname, "The Wall."

"Are you really?"

"I have to be." She looked up and met his gaze, trying to pretend her heart wasn't pounding too hard, and if it was, that it had nothing whatsoever to do with him standing so near. "Okay, thanks for coming. You can go now."

She turned her back on him and resolutely walked to the door and opened it. "Goodbye, Leo."

He hesitated a moment, then nodded and joined her at the exit. "Good night. I know how much you'll miss him. I'm very sorry for your loss."

His voice was so gentle, soft and sincere, yet somehow it popped the bubble of strength around her. She just couldn't keep it up any longer. Moisture blurred her eyes, and big, fat tears rolled down her face. Then the sobbing started, deep, wrenching cries that broke loose from inside her. She covered her face with her hands. If there was anyone she didn't want to see her like this, it was Leo Wallace.

"Tess?"

She couldn't answer, not even to tell him to go away and leave her alone. A moment later she heard the door close and the dead bolt click. Then she felt strong arms come around her and she was folded against his body. He made shushing noises, patted her back and mumbled nonsense about everything being okay.

Tess would never be sure when the closeness stopped being about comfort and turned into *awareness*. There was a reason women were drawn to him and right this moment Tess didn't have the reserves of strength to pretend she was different. No matter how ill-advised it might be.

The good news was that she had stopped crying. The bad was that she looked at him and their gazes locked, and suddenly it was hard to breathe. One moment they were staring at each other, the next he was kissing her. And she was kissing him back!

She opened her mouth and he didn't hesitate to accept the invitation. Their tongues dueled and breathing escalated. He threaded his fingers into her hair as their bodies strained even closer. She could feel that he wanted her and she wanted him, too.

"Leo…" There was no mistaking the pleading in her voice.

"Are you sure?" His eyes darkened with intensity as he searched her gaze. "Maybe this isn't—"

"Don't say it."

Right this second she didn't feel sad or lonely and holding on to that bubble of painlessness was vital. For as long as it lasted, she wanted passion to cancel out the grief. She didn't want to think about anything but this. She tugged him closer to the booth and her butt bumped up against the table. Leo lifted her onto it but there was still a question in his eyes.

"Yes," was the single word she said.

That was all he wanted to hear. As she leaned back onto the table, he slid the hem of her black dress up and hooked his fingers in the waistband of her panties. Quickly he slipped them down her thighs, over her knees, letting them fall down her legs until she kicked them off.

And then he was inside of her, filling her completely. There was no room for thinking; all she could do was feel and take what he offered. He moved slowly, thrusting in and out until she wrapped her legs around his hips to draw him in deeper. One more push and the knot of tension in her belly dissolved as pleasure roared through her. When her shuddering stopped, he thrust one more time and then went still, groaning with the power of his own release.

Tess lay there with her eyes closed. She could feel Leo standing between her legs, palms flat on the table. The only sound in the room was their mingled breathing slowly returning to normal. She didn't want to move. She didn't want to talk. She just wanted to hold on to the haze of pleasure and forgetfulness he'd given her.

"Tess?"

And the glow was gone. She opened her eyes and let him take her hands to help her sit up. He smoothed her dress over her thighs and bent to pick up her panties from the wooden floor.

He held them out. "I don't know what to say."

It was the first time she'd ever seen him less than cocky and self-assured. That was a surprise. "Just don't say you're sorry."

"Should I be?"

"No."

"Are you?" he asked. "Sorry about it?"

"It never happened." She so didn't want to talk about this. "You were never here. I don't want to hear about it. We will never speak of this again. And I don't want to ever hear anyone else talk about it. Is that clear?"

"With women nothing is ever clear," he said.

"Then let me point out that I'm not crying anymore." A vision of what she must look like flashed through her mind because she had ugly-cried. Snot and tears and sobs, oh my. "I'm sorry you had to see that."

"At least you weren't alone."

"It would have been so much better if I was." Oh, dear God, what had she done?

"So you do regret it." His mouth pulled tight for a moment.

"No. *It never happened.*"

"Or do you regret that it was me?"

She didn't want to hurt his feelings. Although he didn't seem to extend that courtesy to the plethora of women he took up with and threw away like used tissues. Still, he'd been considerate enough to pay his respects to her grandfather. Pat had always told her to be nice to Leo. He's not a bad guy. Tess could pull it together just this once. After all, there was nothing like hot, unexpected sex to take your mind off grief.

"Leo, it's just that you and I are like oil and water."

"A minute ago we mixed just fine," he said, the cockiness back in all its glory.

"Nothing happened," she reminded him. But heat crept into her cheeks and if there was a God in heaven, Leo couldn't see it in the dim light. Suddenly she was exhausted and her eyes felt puffy and sore from crying. "If it's all the same to you, I'd like to be alone."

"Whatever you want." For a second it looked as if he would say more, but then didn't. He straightened his clothes and went to the front door, steps away. After opening it he said, "See you, Tess."

"When hell freezes over," she whispered, locking the dead bolt behind him.

Six weeks later Leo was surprised when Tess called and asked him to stop by the bar. Where "it" had never happened. He was on his way there now and very curious about what was on her mind. After the night of Pat's funeral, he'd avoided The Pub, respecting Tess's wishes. But he missed the place, missed the older man who'd been more like a father to him than his own.

She wouldn't talk about whatever it was on the phone but he figured she wanted to discuss investing in her business. Not long before he died, Pat had told him it was in trouble and the best hope of saving it for Tess was to take on a partner. He'd heard what she said when he left after the memorial and figured hell must have frozen over. Her call came out of the blue and the only reason she would speak to him was finances.

He pulled his car into the nearly empty lot outside The Pub. The only other vehicle was a small, fuel-efficient one that had a few years on it. Probably Tess's. Anticipation hummed through him and adrenaline started to flow. Not unlike the way he used to feel before a hockey game.

After parking, he turned off the car and exited. "Let's see what the lady has to say."

He walked to the door, where the Closed sign was displayed. Peeking inside, he saw Tess behind the old-fashioned wooden bar with a brass foot rail. She was wiping everything down.

Leo would have to be a moron to miss the fact that she

didn't like him very much. Other than his ex-wife, who was a lying bitch, Tess was the only woman who'd given him the cold shoulder. Maybe he couldn't get her off his mind because she was a challenge. Without hockey to consume his competitive nature, he was channeling it to her.

That was as good an explanation as any because she wasn't his type. She was pretty enough, but not the kind of woman who gave men whiplash turning to stare. But there was something fresh and appealing about her brown hair and eyes, something friendly and inviting. For everyone but him. Until that night he'd never made a move on her. Why waste time on a woman who showed no sign of ever warming up when an abundance of ladies lined up to be photographed on his arm?

Except she did warm up to him that night. She could pretend it never happened, but he had the scorch marks to prove her wrong.

Time to get his head on straight and talk business. He tried the door and found it was unlocked. Tess looked up but her expression didn't signal that she was happy to see him.

"Hey," he said, closing the door behind him.

"Leo." She stopped wiping the bar and watched him walk over and sit on one of the stools in front of her.

He could almost feel the tension radiating from her. Maybe he could put her at ease. "I want you to know that I respect what you said that night—"

She held up a hand to stop him. "Don't."

"Understood." He met her gaze. "So, why did you ask me to come over and talk?"

"It's about The Pub—" Her lips trembled for a moment as grief slid into her eyes. She blew out a breath and continued, "I'm aware that Granddad came to you with a proposition to invest."

"That's right. I talked with him a lot when I suddenly couldn't play hockey anymore. About what I was going to do." That had been a personal low. He was dealing with an injury that forced him to retire prematurely from the sport that defined him at the same time his wife admitted she'd been cheating with a former lover. She announced she was leaving and taking their child with her. Leo had spent a lot of time at The Pub, drinking and spilling his guts to Patrick. "Your grandfather told me I needed an act two and I had a good head for business. He was right about both."

"He told me you bought the local ice rink and it was finally turning a profit."

"Yes. Among other ventures." All of them had been going down when he took over. Now every one of them was prospering.

"Before I make my pitch, you should know that The Pub was doing fine until Granddad got sick. The medical bills after he was diagnosed were substantial. Even then things were okay. But recently—"

"So you're letting me know you're a good manager."

"Yes. And the good news is that there's been an uptick in business."

"Yet you're approaching me, I assume for help, even though you fought Pat tooth and nail when he suggested I put up money and lend my name to improve declining revenue." At her surprised look he added, "Yeah, he told me you weren't in favor of partnering with me. So why now, Tess?"

"I had to let a full-time employee go and cut hours for others. That's enough to keep the doors open but not to grow." She didn't exactly answer the question of what had changed.

"Okay."

"This place has been my home since I was six and came to live with Granddad. I grew up here. Did my homework in the office in the back. Swept floors because I wanted to help. Did inventory. But there's a lot of debt from his cancer treatment and medical bills. I want his legacy to go on. I just don't want to see it turned into a sports freak show."

He winced at the dig to his former profession but sympathized with the sentiment. Or maybe the sheen of unshed tears in her eyes and the fierce pride on her face made him go soft.

"So, tell me what you're proposing."

She outlined the high points: an infusion of capital to update the place, a percentage of the business and a few other things. She finished up with, "If that's acceptable, I'll take you on as a silent partner."

What she outlined was agreeable to him and at this point in the negotiations it was probably best not to tell her "silent partner" was never going to happen. The thing was he really wanted to buy in. The place was conveniently located and had a lot of potential. Leo also wanted to preserve Pat's life's work.

"Do you have any objection to using my lawyer to draw up a contract?" he asked.

"No."

"Okay, then. I'll get in touch with her first thing in the morning."

"Figures your attorney would be a her."

"I didn't hire Annabel because of her gender. She's a damn good lawyer." And beautiful, too. But it was strictly business and a line he wouldn't cross even if there was an attraction between them.

"If you say so."

Tess was starting to get under his skin, and not in a good way. "Clearly you have a low opinion of me. Why is that?"

"The parade of women through your life for one thing. That speaks to being shallow, self-centered and commitment resistant."

Any guy would run in the face of commitment if he'd been through what Leo had. A guy would have to be an idiot to go through that again. Hockey had given him highs and lows—sanctuary from a lousy home situation, a college education and more than one Stanley Cup championship. The game was physically aggressive and injuries left marks. But they were nothing compared to what losing his career and family at the same time had done to him.

It was best to change the subject and get back to business. "You said The Pub was doing all right until recently. What changed?"

She suddenly looked nervous. "I probably should have led with this, but I wanted to get business details wrapped up first. Although if you have a problem with the fact that I didn't tell you this up front, feel free to change your mind about investing. You don't have to help if you don't want to."

He'd promised Pat he would look after Tess whether she wanted him to or not. There was no way to know what was going through Pat's mind when he made Leo swear, but a vow was a vow. If she was trying to scare him away, it wasn't going to work. "You're not making any sense."

"I know. I just want to make it clear that I'll figure out some other way. I could have worked eighteen hours a day with little pay before and it would have been all right. But things have changed. Now I have to—"

"Tess." That stopped her babbling but not the tension and nerves still making her twist her fingers together. "What's going on?"

She blew out a breath and stood a little straighter, as if bracing herself. "You know that thing we're not talking about that never happened?"

"For the record you can pretend we didn't have sex on that table over there. You can semantics the hell out of it, but that won't change anything. The fact is that we did it. You can bury your head in the sand but that leaves your backside exposed."

"You're not wrong about that." She looked everywhere but at him.

This was really starting to get on his nerves. "What's going on, Tess? Just spit it out."

"I'm pregnant."

He blinked at her and couldn't wrap his mind around the words. "I'm sorry. What?"

"I'm going to have a baby."

Bingo. That was the scariest thing she could have said to him. He couldn't believe it. No way this was happening to him. Not again. He wasn't getting sucked in for a second time by a woman who was lying about having his baby. Leo stood up and walked out of the bar.

Chapter Two

The door closed behind Leo, and Tess could almost feel the sting of a slap on her face. She couldn't decide if she was more shocked or angry that he'd walked out on her. And his child. This was the man her grandfather had wanted as a partner? She'd had her reasons for pushing back on that but none of them were about him not taking responsibility for his actions.

It was about the revolving door of females in and out of his life. Well-publicized, short-term affairs with actresses and models. Glorified one-night stands with glamorous women, rich and famous. Even the not so famous made headlines with him. But in all the publicity surrounding his "over in fifteen minutes" relationships, he'd invariably taken the blame for why things hadn't worked out. Always a version of "she's a great girl and I'm not good enough for her."

As much as she wanted to believe he had no feelings and hurt women from coast to coast when he threw them away, the only one he trashed was himself. One had to conclude he wasn't mean; he just had a problem with commitment. She wasn't into it either. That's what happened when the man you loved cheated repeatedly. He was a cocky college jock and that baggage had affected her opinion of Leo from the moment they were introduced.

In a way, Tess respected the way he characterized the

end of his affairs, even if she didn't condone "quantity over quality" behavior. So yeah, she was more shocked than angry right now. All the scenarios she'd imagined of how this conversation would go down never included him turning his back and walking away.

Tears filled her eyes and she didn't miss the irony. The last time she'd cried in this room, Leo had been there to comfort her and they'd had sex. Now there was a baby and he left her, taking his investment money with him.

Suddenly the door opened and Leo walked back inside. He stood there, staring at her, eyes narrowed dangerously. "A baby. You're sure."

"Peed on a stick and confirmed by a doctor." She had questions, too. "Why did you walk out just now?"

An angry, intense look pulled his mouth tight and made his eyes narrow on her. "I had to think before saying anything."

"Okay. So what are you thinking?"

"Is it mine?"

She was sorry she'd asked. The question tweaked her temper, implying that she was an underhanded opportunist. He was questioning her integrity, but she grudgingly admitted that he had a right to ask. "Yes."

"How do I know it's mine?"

"Because I said so and I don't lie." She glared at him.

He finally closed the door. "Right now, for the sake of argument, let's assume it's mine—"

"Stop calling me a liar. Of course this baby is yours. I've been pretty busy trying to save this bar, my grandfather's legacy. When would I have time to date?"

"You don't have to date," he said wryly.

"That's where you're wrong. I would have to date before doing…" As soon as she realized what was going to come out of her mouth, she stopped talking.

"You and I never went out before we…" He glanced at the booth by the door, where they'd done the deed. Then one corner of his mouth curved up as he looked back at her. "But wait, I forgot. That never happened."

"Obviously you don't intend to let me forget I said that."

"Not likely." He moved closer, stopping on the other side of the bar from her. "You're going to have it." It wasn't a question.

The part of her that wasn't super annoyed with him respected that he wasn't pushing for termination of the pregnancy. Truthfully, that had never entered her mind. "Not that you get to tell me what to do, but yes, I will have this baby."

"I need a test."

To make sure he was the father. As infuriating as it was to be doubted, she'd actually anticipated this. At her first doctor's appointment, she'd asked questions about prenatal testing.

"Before the baby's born it would require an amniocentesis to determine paternity. It's an invasive procedure that requires insertion of a needle to take amniotic fluid. This test poses the risk of miscarriage."

"Okay." His frown deepened. "So we have to wait."

"No. There's a blood test that can determine a very high probability that you're the father. Even though I'm telling you that."

"Like I said. I need a test. Let's do that."

"Okay." She folded her arms over her chest and met his gaze. "I'll set it up. We can have results in one to two days."

"Either you're a very good bluffer or—"

"I'm telling the truth," she finished for him. "Look, Leo, I didn't plan this."

"Okay."

"I can tell that's what you're thinking. I guess if I was in your shoes, the thought would cross my mind."

"Very understanding of you."

"I don't know what to say. I've never been in a situation like this," she defended herself. "It's not like I did it on purpose."

She glanced past him to the booth where it had happened. Heat slid into her cheeks as memories rolled through her mind. Those passionate moments in his arms were all that stood between her and the overwhelming grief of losing her grandfather. She'd never felt so out of control but she couldn't speak for Leo.

"You've had a lot more experience at that sort of thing than me. Since the responsibility should be shared equally, I won't ask why you never brought up the subject of protection."

He shifted his feet, the only sign that her comment struck a nerve. "That's fair. If—"

"I'm telling the truth," she finished. "I never planned to get pregnant. I was upset. I just buried my grandfather and that was a long, horrible day. I'm sorry I couldn't hold back the tears any longer. For the record I didn't ask you to comfort me. In fact I thought I was alone."

A hint of sympathy softened his gaze for a moment. "You weren't. And I assumed you were on birth control."

"I wasn't. And you know what they say about people who assume. Makes an ass out of you and me."

That was an understatement. He and his consolation had taken up every square inch of her attention. And now she was paying a really high price for it.

"I had a lot on my mind that day." She looked around the room. There were pictures on the walls of The Pub while it was being built. Opening day. The surrounding area before homes and businesses popped up. Her glance settled on the wood floor, the scarred bar between them, every mark with a story that was part of the history. "I grew up here with my grandfather. I live in the apartment upstairs. This is my home, as well as my livelihood. My business. My career. It's everything. You've got no skin in the game. Not really. To you it's just an investment."

"Which you're against."

"But Granddad trusted you. And I think you would understand why I feel that way if you were in my situation. For a few weeks after losing Granddad, my bottom line improved." Although that probably had more to do with cutbacks than actual customer expansion. "I thought I could make it. Cost reductions saved money but required me to work more hours."

"Then you found out you were pregnant."

She nodded. "I can't put in the time necessary to keep the business afloat. I have to take care of the baby. And I don't want my grandfather's legacy to disappear, but—"

"So it's the pregnancy that changed your mind about contacting me."

She'd vehemently told him she wasn't a liar. There was no point in starting now. "Yes."

"Because it's the only way to save The Pub."

"Maybe there's another investor I could interest. But Granddad liked you." She would give anything to know why. If only she shared the opinion. She didn't have a problem with him professionally. It was the personal that she was afraid of. Look what happened that night. But there was so much more at stake here. And she didn't have a lot of choices. The only thing she trusted unconditionally was her grandfather's judgment. Other than warm memories and this business, there was nothing left of him. And the thought of it ceasing to exist broke her heart. "Are you still going to invest in the bar?"

"You're having the baby."

"How many times do I have to repeat it? The child I'm carrying is the only reason I need your help. If I wasn't pregnant I'd muddle through without you. Yes, I'm having the baby."

"Then I'm definitely going through with our deal. I'll contact my lawyer to draw up papers."

"I'll make an appointment for blood tests at a private lab."

"Fair enough."

"Okay, then."

She said that with way more enthusiasm than she felt. He obviously didn't believe her about the baby, and the juxtaposition of his agreement implied that if he had no connection to the child, she and her business could dry up and blow away. He was sticking around just to keep her honest.

She couldn't wait to see the look on his face when he had to admit he was wrong about her.

Leo offered to pick Tess up for the meeting at his attorney's office to sign the partnership agreement but she politely declined. In a very cool and distant tone, she'd said it would be best to meet there. Fine with him. He hadn't seen her for a couple of weeks and that was for the best. A cooling-off period gave him time to brace himself to deal with her as they saved her bar. But out of sight didn't mean she was out of his mind. Her and the baby. Damn.

He rode the eight-story building's elevator to the top floor, where Annabel Sanders had her office. The doors opened into the reception area with a view of the whole valley. Huntington Hills in Southern California had a population right around two hundred thousand and was beautiful in the spring. Trees and flowers were blooming, and the vibrant colors of purple, pink and yellow stretched all the way to the mountains.

He walked over to the receptionist. "Hi, Geraldine."

"Mr. Wallace." The attractive woman was in her fifties and had stylishly cut short blond hair. Her blue eyes twinkled with humor. "And you know perfectly well the name is Geri."

"Right. I keep forgetting."

"It's a common problem with our former-hockey-player clients. Too many shots to the head."

"How many hockey-playing clients does Annabel have?"

"Only you. Thank goodness."

"Ah. Maybe I can shake the bushes, contact some of my teammates. Send some business your way."

"Please don't. You keep us busy enough. What with all the investment opportunities you're researching."

He had to make up for lost time. His career ended abruptly, and not long after his marriage ended, too. It was a dark period, most of which he'd spent in Pat Morrow's penalty box. He owed that man a lot for pulling his head out of his ass.

"You know you love me," he said. "If you weren't already happily married…"

She leaned back in her chair and looked up at him. "You're a shameless flirt. I should leave my husband and call your bluff."

"You should. But we both know you won't. You're way too smart to toss aside a good man for the likes of me." Leo felt someone behind him and turned. "Tess. Hi."

"Leo."

"I didn't hear you." No doubt she heard Geri calling him out on his crap.

She ignored him and smiled at the receptionist. "Hello. Tess Morrow to see Annabel Sanders."

"Nice to meet you." Geri gave her the friendly receptionist look. "Annabel is with a client. Her meeting is running a little late. I apologize for that. If you'll just have a seat in the waiting area, she'll be with you both as soon as possible."

"Thanks," Tess answered.

"May I get you something? Coffee?"

"No."

Leo noticed her already pale face go a little whiter. "You okay?"

"Fine." She smiled at Geri, then walked over to the cushy chairs by the windows and sat.

Leo followed and took the seat at a right angle to hers. Because she'd told him she was pregnant, he knew she was nauseated from morning sickness. He still couldn't quite wrap his head around the fact that the baby was his. Maybe.

"So, I got the results of the blood tests," he said.

"Me, too." There was a "told you so" look in her brown eyes.

"It's not conclusive," he pointed out.

"It conclusively confirmed you can't be excluded as the biological father."

She was right about that. He'd done the research. The most accurate results came from an infant's umbilical blood or tissue from the placenta, and that would have to wait another seven or so months. Fetal DNA could be observed in the mother's blood and rule out someone who absolutely couldn't be the father. Right now the test results were not admissible in court for purposes of custody or child support.

But they prevented a guy from getting emotionally involved for months only to find out he had no biological connection. And sometimes a man was led to believe he was a father for several years before finding out he wasn't. He didn't intend to be that naive a second time.

"Leo? Are you all right?"

"Hmm?" He met Tess's questioning gaze.

"You look weird."

Not surprising. He was remembering a weird, painful time in his life. It still hurt and he'd be damned if he'd let another woman pass off another man's child as his. "I'm fine. But I was going to say the same about you. You're a little pale."

"It occurs to me the term *morning sickness* is inaccurate. This icky feeling doesn't just happen in the morning. It can be anytime, day or night."

"So that's why you turned green when Geri mentioned coffee."

"I thought I did a good job of hiding it," she said.

"No." She might be concealing other relevant facts, but not her current distaste for coffee. "But you're not supposed to have it anyway, at least not much," he qualified. "It's not a complete no on caffeine, but it has to be less than two hundred milligrams a day…" He stopped because she was staring at him as if he'd grown another head. "What?"

"How did you know that about coffee during pregnancy?"

He knew because he'd married the last woman who said she was having his baby and embraced the experience with her. Along with the pain of finding out the son he loved more than life wasn't his, he remembered pregnancy do's and don'ts. "I guess I just heard it somewhere."

"You do meet a lot of women." There was sarcasm in her voice.

"One of the perks of being a hockey star," he said, hoping to change the focus of this conversation.

"Must be a difficult cross to bear." Now bitterness mixed with the sarcasm.

If he didn't know better, he would say she was a little bit jealous, but that proved again just how bad he was at reading women. She'd taken a dislike to him almost from the moment they met. There was definite female interest in her eyes, right up until Pat Morrow introduced him as a former professional hockey player. *An athlete*, she'd said, in a disdainful tone that lumped him in with litterbugs and dog haters. Neither of which he was.

He'd liked her from the first but she gave him the cold shoulder. Until the night of her grandfather's memorial service, when she was hot as hell and took him to heaven. She was right about one thing. He had had no room in his brain to think about protection that night. Holding her felt that good. *If* the baby was his, the blame could be shared fifty-fifty. But that night proved one thing. Tess was attracted to him even though she disapproved of him personally.

He met her gaze. "I do like women. That's not a hanging offense."

"No one said it was."

"You didn't have to say it. Judgment is written all over your face."

"Wow," she said. "Apparently my face gives away more than just the fact that the thought of coffee makes me want to barf."

"Was it coffee? I assumed it was the sight of me."

"Wow again. I'm surprised you could find a helmet big enough for your swelled head. Not everything is about you, Leo."

"And jumping to that conclusion just proves—"

"Hello, Leo." His attorney interrupted him. The pretty, green-eyed redhead smiled at Tess and held out her hand. "I'm Annabel Sanders. You must be Ms. Morrow."

"Tess." She shook the other woman's hand.

"I apologize for keeping you waiting. I didn't expect my last client to take as long as he did."

"I didn't see him leave," Leo said.

"I'm not surprised. You were having an intense chat." Annabel's eyes narrowed on him for a moment, and then she smiled at Tess. "It's nice to meet you."

As the two women chatted, Leo studied his lawyer. She was a beautiful woman. Spectacular curves were showcased in the body-hugging hunter green dress with the flaring skirt. She was also funny and brilliant but he'd never felt the slightest hint of attraction to her. Not once in the nearly two years he'd known her. Maybe because their relationship was professional.

"If you'll both follow me into my office, we can go over the agreement."

He let the women precede him into the large corner office with floor-to-ceiling windows on two sides. In one corner was a conversation area, defined by a leather love seat, two matching club chairs and a glass coffee table. The attorney sat behind her large desk. These digs were much nicer than the small, cramped office where they'd had their very first meeting.

Annabel opened a file on her desk and put on her lawyer face. "Tess, you got the email I sent with the attachment containing the agreement?"

"Yes."

"You had a chance to read it over and have your attorney look at it?"

"I read it," Tess said. "It looks fine to me."

Leo had clued Annabel in on the background that the partnership was a go because Tess was strapped for cash and trying to save her business. He could see her making that connection as the reasoning for not getting a second legal opinion.

"I can assure you that the terms are extremely fair," Annabel told her.

Tess nodded. "I agree."

"Do you have any questions?"

"No."

The attorney nodded. "Leo was very clear that he didn't want to take advantage of your grief and your grandfather's passing. My condolences, by the way."

"Thank you." Tess glanced at him and the paleness in her cheeks disappeared, replaced by a charming pink. Must be the "taking advantage" comment.

As he saw it, they'd had a mutual taking advantage, and the memories were never far from his mind.

"The thing is, Ms. Sanders—"

"Annabel, please."

"Okay. Annabel. Before he died, my grandfather approached Leo about the partnership because he trusted him. I have faith in his judgment. And I didn't see anything in the paperwork that changed my mind."

"Okay, then. We'll get this done."

She went through each page, having them sign and initial where indicated. It was a lot of paperwork, but finally they reached the end.

"Congratulations," the attorney said. "You two have a partnership."

"In business," Tess clarified.

"Yes." Annabel looked from one to the other. "By definition partners need to work together."

"Are you lecturing us?" Leo asked.

"No. Yes. Maybe." She looked at him. "I heard you talking in the waiting room and got the feeling there's an adversarial aspect to your relationship. If you're going to make a success of this venture, it's important to work together."

"Of course," he said.

"I mean it." She looked at Tess. "I don't know you, but I've worked with Leo for several years. He has an excellent head for business and a successful track record to prove it. Don't let his cocky attitude fool you."

"If you say so," Tess said defensively. "I should point out that I'm no slouch. I have a degree in business and I've worked at the bar my whole life. There's a loyal core of customers and we have to build on it."

"That's the plan," Leo agreed.

"Okay. I didn't mean to overstep, but I see the other side when things don't work out. I dissolve partnerships, too."

"Our joint venture will be fine," Leo assured her. It was also necessary. "So, Tess, I'll come by The Pub in the morning and we'll discuss strategy?"

"Fine."

"Is nine too early?"

"No." But she looked as if she had swallowed a worm.

He'd never expected to go into business with Tess Morrow. But now that she was allegedly carrying his child, it was the best way to keep tabs on her. If she slipped up, he would be around to call her on the deception.

The last time he got screwed, he lost everything. He wasn't so gullible now. He would do whatever he had to in order to protect himself.

Chapter Three

Morning sickness really sucked!

It especially sucked when Tess had to see Leo bright and early. The early part she could do. Bright? Not so much. But he would be arriving at nine o'clock sharp and she needed to look her best. Well, at least the best she could what with feeling like something the cat yakked up.

She showered, put on makeup and blew her hair dry. Unlike her unruly tummy, it cooperated, falling past her shoulders in its shiny straightness.

She stared at her reflection in the bathroom mirror and ignored the dark circles under her eyes. "You look fabulous. This will be the first of many productive and profitable meetings."

She managed to choke down a piece of toast with peanut butter. The doctor had said to eat lots of protein but she'd never expected that to be such a challenge. Five minutes before nine o'clock, she walked downstairs from her apartment. The staircase ended in a hall where a left turn went to public restrooms and the bar. Going right would put her in the office and storeroom, with high-capacity refrigeration, an ice maker and shelves. She went left.

In the bar, chairs were turned upside down on tables, where they always spent the night. There were two more rooms off the main area—one for pool and darts, the other with tables for a quieter space for grabbing a bite to eat. Some people might still enjoy eating even though she wasn't one of them right now.

A knock on the door pulled her from the brink of self-pity and she moved to let Leo in. "Good morning."

"Hi." He handed her a bag.

"What's this?"

"Thought these might come in handy."

She peeked inside and saw soda crackers. "Wow. Be still my heart."

"What were you expecting?"

"Nothing actually. So, thanks."

"Keep them by the bed and eat one before you get up. It helps with morning sickness."

"And you know this how?"

He shrugged. "I picked up the information somewhere."

"It's unexpectedly thoughtful, so I won't say anything snarky about your women clueing you in."

"That's very generous of you." One corner of his mouth quirked up. Then he indicated the briefcase he was holding. "I've been consulting with a building contractor—"

"Wait." She held up a hand to stop him. "We only just signed the papers yesterday."

"Since our verbal agreement, I talked to someone I've worked with on other business ventures. The guy is creative and does great work. He came up with some changes and I happen to think they'll be a better use of the space we have."

We? Apparently just signing the papers didn't make her a team player. But since she'd put her name on the bottom line, telling him to take a flying leap didn't seem like something she could do.

"Okay. Show me." She grabbed one of the chairs from a table to make room for a conversation with visual aids.

"You shouldn't be lifting things."

"Why not? I'm fine. Just pregnant—not an invalid." She rested her hands on her hips. "If not me, who's going to lift things?"

"Not while I'm around." He set down his briefcase, then removed the other three chairs.

"Thanks."

There he went being sweet again. That was twice in one morning. Tess didn't trust sweet. It was easy to heft chairs and bring crackers, but a man like him couldn't keep up sweet for long.

They sat and he pulled out his laptop, then set it on the table. He opened a file and then slid his chair closer to hers so they could view the screen together. He smelled good, disarmingly masculine. Some combination of soap and cologne that made her tummy flutter—with something besides nausea. It was attraction, damn him. That's what had gotten her into this mess in the first place, and still fascination survived. There was something seriously wrong with her that she couldn't shake this feeling.

"Okay. So, what am I looking at?"

"This is what the bar would look like with the two walls knocked out, making it one big room."

Not ten minutes ago she'd been thinking how cozy and perfect the setup was with quiet dining and game rooms separated. "But what about the pool tables and dart boards? And some people like a peaceful corner for food and conversation."

"A few customers might appreciate that. If they don't like the change, there are quiet restaurants to take their business. That isn't our core customer, not the clientele we want to attract."

"We can't afford to lose anyone."

"We'll more than make up for that with new business.

Look at the way Nate has it drawn out. The tables are still there. And we'll add an air-hockey table to the game area."

"We will?" She shifted and their arms brushed. The touch made her hot all over but he didn't seem to notice.

"Hockey is trendy."

"Pool is classic."

"We can do both. Open that customer-interest window wider." He met her gaze and something intense flared in his when his knee grazed hers under the table.

Not unlike the way he'd looked at her the night *it* had happened. She swallowed and forced herself to look at the computer screen. She pointed to the opposite corner.

"What's this?"

"We took some of the dining space for live music and dancing. On the weekends people want to de-stress."

"You mean relax."

"I mean let off steam. Loud music. Singing. Maybe karaoke. Watching games and yelling at their team or booing the opponent. Dancing. Contests. Promotions."

He was so enthusiastic but she was looking at the end of an era and it made her sad. "Did my grandfather know about any of this?"

"I talked to him a little bit. Brainstormed as ideas popped into my head."

"What did he say?"

"Pretty much what you are," he admitted. "But he didn't shoot anything down. He knew status quo wasn't working."

That was honest. He could have lied. Pat Morrow was gone and she'd never know what he thought. She couldn't dispute that the current situation was less than successful, but she wasn't ready to concede the point yet.

"Would you like some coffee?" It was a delaying tactic, giving her more time to think.

"Yeah. If it's not too much trouble."

"There's a pot right here." She needed to put some distance between them and was willing to risk the smell.

She went behind the bar and put water and grounds into the drip coffee maker, then hit the on switch. When there was nothing left to do but wait, she walked back to the table, careful to stand far enough away so that she couldn't be distracted by his body heat and manly smell.

As if there'd been no pause, Leo started talking. "We need to put in TVs around the room to show football, baseball, hockey games. Make this the designated place to watch my former team."

"Lend your celebrity name to bring in customers?" She meant women but kept that to herself.

"Yes. Anything that will get the word out there so people will give us a try."

"I don't know about this, Leo." She frowned. Apparently he'd forgotten what she'd said about turning her grandfather's legacy into a sports freak show.

"Look, Tess, I'm aware that this is an emotional time for you—"

"Hold the phone. Don't make my hesitation about me being pregnant. I have a business degree with a minor in marketing."

"That's not what I meant. Your grandfather just died and this pub was his baby. He put everything he had into every corner. But he knew that change isn't a bad thing. We can make it fresh and still keep his heart and soul. You just have to trust me."

And there was the problem. He was too much like the guy who had broken her heart, which made trust in his judgment hard to come by. But that was personal. This was business and his lawyer had assured her he was good at it. Plus her grandfather had chosen him to invest.

While they'd debated, coffee brewed and the smell of it was everywhere. Or maybe it was her supersensitive nose due to pregnancy. Didn't matter why, but the stronger the smell, the worse she felt. She fought back as long as possible but it was a losing battle.

"I'm—oh, God—I'm going to be sick."

She put her hand over her mouth and raced upstairs for the privacy of her own bathroom. She made it—barely—and lost her breakfast. No way the perfect Leo Wallace was going to see her toss her cookies.

"Tess?"

Dear God, no. He followed her! "Go away."

The next thing she knew, he was beside her, scooping her hair back from her face as she bent over the toilet. She'd be furious if she didn't feel hot, sweaty and humiliated. He held her hair with one hand and rubbed her back with the other.

No, no, no. "Go away. Please," she mumbled.

"Not happening."

Her stomach was empty but she waited a few moments to make sure it was over. With a shaking hand, she pressed the handle to flush and then straightened up. After closing the lid, she stood and sat down on it, refusing to meet his gaze.

"I'm okay now. Really. You can go. I'll meet you downstairs in a minute."

Her eyes drifted shut, but she heard the sound of running water in the sink. A moment later he pressed a cool washcloth to her forehead and rubbed it across her neck. It felt so good she could cry. That might be about gratitude, or hormones, or both.

"Stay here. I'll be back in a second."

Before she could pull together the energy to say "don't tell me what to do," he was gone. Several moments later he was back with the box of crackers. He opened it and one of the four individual packs inside, then handed her a salty square.

"This will help." He crouched in front of her so they were eye to eye. His were full of sweetness and sympathy.

"The last thing I want to do is eat," she said weakly.

"I know, but you have to. This will settle your stomach."

If she didn't feel so crappy, she would have asked how he could be so sure. Instead she gave him a skeptical look. "If you're wrong and I lose it again, will you promise to go away?"

"Cross my heart."

"Do you have one?" She took a small bite of cracker, chewed and swallowed.

"There's the snark I know and love. You must be feeling a little better."

When there was no adverse reaction to the single nibble, she took another and waited. It went down easily. Even more surprising, she was suddenly hungry. "Can I have another one?"

He handed her the package. "Knock yourself out."

She took small bites and chewed slowly. "You know, when I took the pregnancy test and it was positive, I couldn't believe it was true. There was nothing tangible to prove I was going to have a baby. Then bam. I feel like roadkill, proof that there are changes going on."

"Nature is pretty amazing."

She nibbled two more crackers and began to feel more like herself. She knew that because her defenses against him were going back up.

"You're being awfully nice to me for a man who doesn't believe this baby is his."

He looked down for a second, then back at her. There

was a glint of humor in his blue eyes. "About that… I asked around, to see if you'd slept with anyone else."

"You didn't!"

"Everyone said no. But you might have said it never happened."

"Okay. Now you're being a jerk so all is right with the world." But was it? Her heart seemed to swell a couple of sizes. "Make no mistake. If it gets out how sweet you're being to me, there will be hell to pay."

"Oh?"

"More women will throw their panties at you."

"More than zero?" He arched an eyebrow. "No one does that now."

"Like I believe that," she scoffed.

But she couldn't shrug off how incredibly nice he was being, even with questions still surrounding the pregnancy. She didn't think he had a sweet bone in his body. But she was wrong and that was a problem.

Leo stood outside The Pub, waiting for Tess to let him in for their meeting with the contractor. Nate Stratton would be here any minute, and Leo wanted a few moments to reassure her, yet again, that the changes would be profitable in the long run. Which was what her grandfather had ultimately wanted.

He hadn't seen her since the morning a couple of days ago when she'd tossed her cookies. She'd been a trouper then, no question. It wasn't often her vulnerability showed, and she probably hadn't been able to brazen it out. The pregnancy hormones were in charge after all. But, damn, seeing her toughness slip brought out a protectiveness he hadn't experienced since—

The door opened and there she was, looking so pretty and… Dare he say it? Glowing. "Hi."

"Good morning," he managed to say.

She glanced at the store-bought cups of coffee he was holding, one in each hand. "I hope you didn't bring me one. Not after last time."

"No. It's for Nate. So you don't have to make coffee." He'd expected her expression to soften or maybe get a hint of a smile, but her frown deepened. "What?"

"That was very thoughtful of you."

"Then why do you look like that?"

"Like what?" she asked.

"Like you want to brain me with a coffeepot."

"I didn't think it showed," she admitted.

"You lost me."

"You're being nice. Thoughtful. I don't trust it." She shrugged, defiance in her eyes.

At least she was being honest, he thought. "Well, I'm not sure how to defend myself against that. What if I promise not to be nice anymore?"

She nodded approval. "I'd appreciate that."

"Can I come in now?"

"Oh. Sure. Sorry." She stepped back and pulled the door wide. "It's half yours now."

And she wasn't happy about it. The tone, the body language, the glare she tried to hide. All of it said she wasn't yet reconciled to him being her partner. Only financial results would show her this was a good thing, and that wasn't going to happen overnight. Still, he did miss the sexy woman who'd clung to him and kissed him back. He was fighting that feeling because it was dangerous. It would be months until he knew for sure she was telling the truth about the baby. Speaking of which…

"How are you feeling?"

"So far, so good. Today. The crackers are helping."

"Glad to hear it."

"I'm really curious how you know so much about pregnancy nausea." She folded her arms over her chest and looked up at him as if he was breaking some rule.

The truth was his wife was pregnant when they'd married, and he'd gone through it with her. Reading the books. Researching on the internet. Catering to her cravings. It was hard to shake the bitterness about how that had all turned out. Tess's grandfather had helped him deal and obviously hadn't spilled the facts to her, treating Leo's story like attorney/client privilege. That was then; this was now and he didn't want to talk about it.

"I must have seen it in a movie." If only. Then it wouldn't still hurt like a son of a bitch.

"Anyway. Thanks for the tip." She glanced at the watch on her wrist. "Your friend is late."

"He's busy. I had to do some fast talking to get him to take us on." Although now that he thought about it, Nate's attitude had changed a little after meeting Tess and looking at the bar.

"No rush as far as I'm concerned." Translation: she didn't care if it never started.

"That's emotion talking. Because in your business classes I'm sure you learned that the sooner you start increasing profits, the sooner your business is out of trouble."

She nodded. "And the sooner you can turn everything over to me and we'll see less of each other."

Only if the baby wasn't his.

"Since we're going to turn this place into a sports freak show, I suggest lending my name," he said. "It's recognizable."

"To who? Besides your female fans, of course."

"I have two Stanley Cup rings." The look on her face

didn't change, so he said, "You do know the significance of that, right?"

"Actually, no."

"In hockey it's the equivalent of winning the World Series in baseball. Or the Super Bowl in football."

"Ah." She still didn't look impressed.

"And we came close to winning it at least five more times."

"So, lending your name. Does that mean we're going to call it Leo's Lounge or The 'Wall' Flower?"

"Funny." Until now he hadn't been aware that she knew his hockey nickname. "We can talk about names later. I'm more interested in getting the inside ready." He looked at his watch. "And if Nate doesn't get here soon—"

"Knock, knock." The door opened and in walked Nate Stratton, bachelor, builder, businessman. "Sorry I'm late. Had a crisis at another site."

"Glad you made it," Leo said.

"Hi." Tess smiled in a way she'd never smiled at Leo. It was a friendly look, but a little flirty around the edges. She held out her hand. "Nice to see you again."

"Same here." Did the guy hold her hand a little too long when he shook it?

Leo was aware that women found his friend attractive. They'd been each other's wingman more than once, and a time or two his date had made a move on the guy. It never bothered him before but it damn sure did now.

"So, what have you got to show us?" Leo wanted to move this along.

"I've got the plans on the computer." He put it down on the table without chairs on top of it. "Here we go. I think you're really going to like this."

Tess and Leo moved chairs and sat on either side of the contractor. Was she close enough to Nate that their arms brushed? he wondered. The thought did not make him happy.

Nate went through more detailed, three-dimensional plans from the initial one Leo had originally shown Tess. They *were* good. He could easily picture the changes opening up the interior of the bar and infusing life into the place. He glanced at Tess but had no idea what was going through her mind.

"This is just a thought," Leo said. "But since we're doing some makeover anyway, I propose we upgrade the kitchen. We can hire a chef and shake up the menu. Another marketing strategy."

Tess looked less than thrilled. "I feel everything my grandfather put into this place slipping away."

"I promise when I'm finished there will be a mix of old and new," Nate promised. "Not that I get a vote, but I agree with Leo about the kitchen. Atmosphere, fun and good food will bring in the customers."

"Nothing is sacred," Tess muttered.

"If you don't want—" Nate started.

She held up her hand to stop him. "No. If we're going to make changes, let's go all in."

"You won't be disappointed," Leo assured her.

"I agree." Nate looked at each of them. "Let's talk logistics."

The contractor explained how many weeks total for the work, the mess involved and the estimated time frame The Pub would have to close for construction. He gave Leo a copy of the plans on a flash drive and instructions to contact him after they had discussed everything. He would draw up a contract and give them a start date. Then he excused himself to go to another meeting he was already late for.

When they were alone, Tess met his gaze, her own worried. "I didn't think about keeping this place open during construction. Or that it would have to close."

"It's a lot to consider, but remember he said it would only close for a short time. When water and electricity would have to be turned off, we can't conduct business." Leo thought for a moment. "But before that stage, we can have a 'pardon our dust' promotion. Half off drinks and food. Extended happy hour. BOGO. See the before and after. Customers will respond."

"When life gives you lemons, make lemonade?"

"Exactly," he said enthusiastically.

"We can't afford to lose anyone."

"I know. It will be all right. But there's something else that concerns me more than that." He turned his chair toward her, the now-empty one sitting between them.

"What could possibly be worse than shrinking our customer base?" she asked. "Or losing four to six weeks of revenue?"

"Construction means dust and paint fumes in this building."

"Okay. We can utilize the patio area more. Use outside heaters if necessary until summer is here."

"No. I meant I'm concerned about you living upstairs during the demolition and painting. Plus if the water and electricity are off, you can't be here."

"I can make do. I'm tough."

"You're also pregnant. None of that will be healthy for you and the baby."

Now she looked uneasy. "I'll get fans and open the windows upstairs. It's spring. It will be fine."

"I'm not comfortable with that." No matter whose baby she was carrying, the scenario they were discussing was bad.

"It's where I live. What do you want me to do?"

"Move out."

"Where?"

"Can't you couch surf with friends?"

She thought for a moment and then shook her head. "Anyone I'd feel comfortable asking either doesn't have room or is living with a parent."

"Then an extended-stay hotel."

She shook her head. "I'll just have to make this work here at The Pub."

"Why are you pushing back so hard?" he asked.

"Because I don't have the money to stay somewhere else."

"I'll pay for it. The cost of doing business," he explained.

"I can't let you do that."

Her face was showing all kinds of stubborn kicking in, so he didn't pursue that approach. There was one more thing he could think of.

"Move in with me. I don't live with my parents." Heaven forbid. He couldn't wait to get out of that battle zone when he was a kid. "And I have plenty of room at my place. We'd probably never see each other."

"That's not a good idea."

"I disagree. It's the perfect solution. And it won't cost any more out of pocket. So everything is settled. It won't be for long. It'll be great."

The best part was that he could really keep an eye on her. To make sure she ate properly and took care of herself. If he could also see for himself that she wasn't going out with another man that would be okay, too.

Chapter Four

Leo finally wore her down and Tess agreed to move in when The Pub renovation started. It moved quickly, and two weeks later she pulled her small compact car into his circular driveway and parked behind his big, expensive silver SUV. She'd always figured him for something flashier but he'd said they were too small and uncomfortable. The thought of his broad shoulders squeezed into a sports car made her heart flutter more than a little, which was disconcerting since she was practically on his doorstep.

A very impressive doorstep, attached to a New England–style house with gables and siding, surrounded by manicured grass, bushes and flowers. She was a little nervous about seeing the inside. Sharing living space with the man whose outstanding shoulders had just made her heart flutter was definitely going to be something. Whether good or bad was yet to be determined.

She didn't quite know what to make of his inviting her to stay with him. He was right about the dust and paint fumes, though. She'd checked with the doctor, who totally agreed with him. And anyone she'd felt comfortable asking for temporary lodging would have been inconvenienced. Leo sure didn't lie about the size of his place. He could put up the entire UCLA marching band here.

But she had a sneaking suspicion the offer had more to do with not trusting her than anything else.

Trust was a fragile thing. Once broken it was pretty darn hard to rebuild. She found it easiest not to believe in someone at all.

"Enough procrastinating," she said to herself. "Journey of a thousand miles. Single step and all that."

She popped the trunk on her car, then exited and went to the rear to get her suitcases. Before she could, the front door opened and Leo came out and jogged down the three steps.

"Let me get that stuff," he said.

"Thanks." She didn't push back, because somehow he always got his way. Without another word she grabbed a couple of grocery bags out of the rear seat and followed him inside. "Where's the kitchen?"

"Back there." His hands were full so he lifted his chin to indicate the general direction. "I'll take your suitcases up to the guest room."

"Okay. Thanks," she said again.

That was very sweet of him, and the more she got to know him, the more she actually liked Leo Wallace. Since they were now partners, that was a good thing, right? As long as it didn't turn into more than business. Although that seemed like shutting the barn door after the horse got out. And now they would be roomies. Eventually they'd be parenting together. Maybe they could be friends. She was beginning to think she could manage that.

The man had very good taste in houses but the jury was out on his decorating skills, what with the interior having very few furnishings. There was nothing in the living and dining rooms. In the kitchen there were white cabinets and gorgeous granite on an island as big as a Toyota.

The adjacent family room had a flat-screen TV above the fireplace and a brown leather corner group in front of it.

Tess set her bags of groceries on the island and went in search of her host. Walking up the curving staircase she called out, "Leo?"

"Up here."

Following the sound of his voice, she found him in the first bedroom off the upstairs landing. She walked in and looked around. Her suitcases were on a flat bench at the foot of a king-size bed. The spread had flowers and matching throw pillows. Somehow the decor didn't seem to fit a man whose nickname was "The Wall."

"This is a beautiful room." And she meant that sincerely.

There was a window seat that looked out onto the brick patio that surrounded a big pool. A door to her left led to the full bath and big walk-in closet.

"Somehow I didn't picture you as a flowered comforter kind of guy," she said as she turned to him.

He looked a little sheepish and awfully darn cute when he said, "I bought the furniture and bedding after we agreed you would move in."

Her chest tightened and she had the distinct feeling that her heartstrings were being tugged. He was telling her that this room had been empty and he furnished it with decor that was suspiciously similar to that found in her apartment. One could conclude that he'd done it specifically for her. But one really and truly didn't want to believe that.

"It's lovely. And very nice of you. But you promised not to be nice to me."

"Yeah." He shrugged. "I forgot. Want to see the rest of the place?"

"Yes."

She trailed after him from room to room as he explained where everything was and showed her the huge backyard. The grass area beyond the pool was big enough for a hockey rink, if it wasn't Southern California, where it was only possible to maintain indoor ice with equipment. He'd even made space for her in his downstairs office so she had somewhere to work.

Back in the kitchen he showed her around. Last but not least there was a rack hanging over the island with copper-bottom pots and pans dangling from it. The effect was all pretty perfect.

He noticed the bags of groceries sitting there. "What's this?"

"I'm making dinner. My way of contributing."

"You don't have to."

"Are you afraid I can't cook?" she challenged. "You were awfully quick to suggest hiring a chef for The Pub."

"It was just a thought. A brainstorming thing."

"Because the burgers, hot dogs, and fish and chips I make aren't fancy enough?" It was simple stuff and she wasn't the only one who did the cooking. Which reminded her. "It was generous of you to pay the employees while the renovation is underway."

"It's fair. Also smart business to retain good help. Cheaper in the long run since they're already trained," he explained.

"Still, it's appreciated."

He leaned back against the counter and slipped his fingertips into the pockets of his worn jeans. "So, what's for dinner?"

"You'll see."

"Can I help?"

She thought for a moment. "Maybe set the table. And there's stuff in the bags to make salad."

"On it," he said.

She'd brought everything necessary for chicken marsala, including the cooking wine. He gave her a funny look and she got it right away. "The alcohol will burn off in cooking. It's fine for a pregnant lady."

"Okay."

She found her way around his kitchen as if she'd set it up herself, which was a little disconcerting. Their minds, organizationally speaking, worked the same way. That saved her time in fixing dinner. When everything was ready she put the food out on the circular oak table, in a nook with a view of the backyard.

She cut a bite of chicken and nodded as the flavors hit her tongue. "It's not bad, if I do say so myself."

He tried it and met her gaze, surprise in his own. "Definitely a winner."

"Don't sound so shocked. I have skills."

"I'm aware."

There was a hint of something in his voice that she had a feeling meant he wasn't only referring to her cooking abilities. Best not to go there, so they ate in silence. He scarfed up everything on his plate, and then had a second helping. It made her happy that he enjoyed it. Maybe that had something to do with her nesting instincts, which had gone nuts so far in this pregnancy.

"This is really a beautiful home," she said to break the silence. "How long have you lived here?"

"Awhile," he said vaguely.

"Can we talk about how sparse the furnishings are?"

"Nothing to say," he told her. "That hasn't been a priority."

"What has?"

"Business. I needed something to fill my time when I stopped playing hockey."

A career-ending injury must have been hard, she thought. "So investing in businesses keeps you busy?"

"And pays the bills."

Still, she was curious. Was he deliberately not putting down roots? Less stuff equaled a fast getaway?

She wouldn't pry, but couldn't resist needling him about something else. Maybe it was payback because he'd initially walked out on her without a word when she'd told him about the baby.

"So, which room are you going to make the nursery?"

He stopped chewing, then slowly raised his gaze to hers. "What?"

"You'll want to have a place for the baby when he's with you. There are a lot of bedrooms upstairs. Which one are you thinking for him?"

"First of all—*him*?"

"I won't keep saying *it*. So *he*," she explained. "And which room were you thinking of for him?"

Something dark slipped into his eyes. He set his fork on the plate as if he'd suddenly lost his appetite. "I'll figure it out. If necessary."

"It will be," she assured him. "You can't just throw things together at the last minute. God knows I'm starting to freak out a little about all that needs to be done."

"Actually newborns don't need that much. One trip to the store and you're good."

"Really?"

"Yeah. Stuff to change diapers. Onesies. A few sleepers. If you breastfeed, you don't even need bottles. The rest of it you can get as needed."

"What about a crib?"

"Babies don't move around much for the first couple of months." He shrugged.

This made her more curious than the sparse furnishings in his house. Forget the fact that he provided soda crackers for morning sickness. "How do you know so much about babies?"

"Good question. Guys on the team had kids. I guess some of what they said sank in." The casual tone was forced and his eyes never lost their sort of tense, haunted look.

She didn't buy his explanation. In her experience men just didn't have much information about infant care. What was his story? As badly as she wanted to ask, she didn't go there.

She met his gaze and decided not to bring up breastfeeding. "We're going to need bottles for him. You'll need them when he's with you."

"If," he reminded her.

She was annoyed because she knew he was the only one who could be the father of her baby. But he was at a disadvantage; he didn't know for sure that she'd only been with him. So she cut him some slack.

"You're really stubborn. Your resistance to this child being yours is impressive."

"I'm not resisting, just waiting it out."

"Okay. But I'm telling you your life is going to change. Half the time you're going to be responsible for a baby. Feeding. Changing diapers."

"So will you," he said.

She didn't need the reminder. Nerves about how this was going to alter her life were already starting. She was just spreading the joy. "It occurs to me that at least half the time you're going to have to put the brakes on your love life. Assuming the flavor of the month isn't into children."

"Same goes for you." He wasn't smiling.

"I have no love life to interrupt," she told him.

"Really?" There was a glimmer of curiosity in his eyes that finally chased away the dark look. "I would think a lot of guys are interested."

"I meet a lot," she admitted. "It's part of the job. Some hit on me."

"And?"

"Nothing." She wasn't interested.

"Not that I believe it, but why?"

"It's like picking out a dog." She thought about how that sounded. "I don't mean all guys are dogs but when choosing, you don't want the one that's all over you. They're too eager. The one that hangs back is more calm and centered. Trainable."

"I see." He looked amused.

"My point is, are you sure you want me here? If you're bringing a woman home, you can just let me know. I'll make myself scarce."

"That won't be necessary," he said wryly.

"Right. Because you can always go to her place."

"No. Because there are no women."

When he got up and started clearing plates, it was clear the discussion was over. But that didn't stop her mind from racing.

Now that she thought about it, Leo had hung back until the night of her grandfather's memorial. To be fair, for some reason they'd both melted down simultaneously, and there was no explaining it because she would never be his flavor of the month. But they would always be connected by this child she was carrying.

And he knew an awful lot about pregnant women and infants. It seemed odd that he even knew what a onesie was. The man had a story, a secret, and she wanted to know what it was.

There was a woman in the house. Tess.

A woman he hadn't slept with the night before, which happened now and then. Leo wished he could say he had no interest in sleeping with her, except he did. But that wasn't an option because they were in business together. If that wasn't enough, sex would complicate an already bad situation. He didn't trust that she was telling the truth, even though she seemed completely confident that he was the baby's father.

In case she wasn't lying, he was going to make sure she didn't sleep in a building full of demolition dust and paint fumes. And that she ate well—for both her and the baby.

So this morning he cut up fresh fruit and made an egg, cheese and potato casserole. It was easy and good. He hoped Tess would like it. More specifically he hoped it wouldn't make her throw up.

He glanced at the clock on the microwave again and noted that the morning was slipping away. Did she normally sleep late? Possibly, since The Pub was busiest at night. But what if she wasn't okay? This house was big and he might not have heard if she needed help. Should he check on her? Maybe send a text? She'd taken her phone upstairs with her. If she didn't answer, he would go up and knock—

"Good morning."

He was checking on breakfast in the oven, and at the sound of her voice he closed the door and turned. "Hey, sleepyhead."

"I'm sorry I slept so late, but that bed is really comfortable. I was out cold."

That made one of them because the sight of her made him hot all over. "I'm glad. Not that you were out. That you slept well."

"I did." She sniffed. "Something smells good."

"Breakfast."

"A man who cooks," she commented.

"I'm a bachelor. Someone has to."

He told her what was in it and then studied her for signs that the scents of food were not adversely affecting her. He didn't see anything in her bright brown eyes and sunny smile that said she needed crackers. There was a fresh-faced prettiness about her that he'd liked the first time they had met.

And he was going to do his best to ignore how nice it was to have a woman here. He was also ignoring that this was the first time this house felt like a home. It had been a while since a woman spent the night, and he was going to chalk his feelings up to that.

"Are you hungry?" he asked.

"Yes."

"Smell's not bothering you?"

"No. And that's getting better. Everything I read about pregnancy said it usually does right about where I am now."

"Do you think it would be okay for me to make coffee?"

"Yes." She gave him a "don't go being nice to me" look. "Did you not make it because of me?"

"No big deal. I was going to stop by Starbucks later, when I went out."

"That's exactly what I didn't want," she said firmly.

"For me to go to Starbucks?"

"No. To change your routine because I'm here. Let me make coffee."

The determination on her face told him if he challenged her, he would lose the argument. "As long as you're not going to turn green."

"Can't promise," she said. "But if it happens I'll deal."

"Okay. Coffee is in the refrigerator." He nodded toward the machine on the counter. "There's the beast to make it."

"I'm on it."

She rounded the island and moved past him to get started. The scent of her skin lingered in her wake and made him feel light-headed. For a second his brain was as scrambled as the eggs he'd mixed into the casserole. If someone asked his name, he wasn't 100 percent sure he would have remembered it.

"Leo?"

"Hmm?" He forced himself to focus. "Did you say something?"

"How do you like your coffee? Weak. Medium. Or stand a spoon up in it."

"Medium."

"Got it." She measured grounds, added water to the reservoir, then pushed the button. Almost immediately there was the sound of sizzling and dripping into the pot. The smell of coffee was strong in the air and he watched her closely for signs of her hundred-yard dash to the bathroom.

"Would you like me to set the table?" she asked.

"Sure. That would be great."

He watched her reach into the upper cabinet for plates and noticed her short T-shirt ride up, revealing a stretch of creamy bare skin that winked in his direction. The joke was on him. For the second time a woman had told him she was pregnant with his child and he needed to be sure he wouldn't get sucked into the fairy tale again. After his life had fractured, it had taken a while to pull himself out of the pit of darkness. He wouldn't go there twice.

As soon as it was safe, he would move her back to the apartment. In the meantime he'd keep tabs on her, in case she was trying to pull a fast one.

The timer on his phone signaled that the casserole was done. He gave it a once-over and determined it was ready, then grabbed protective mitts and pulled the cast-iron skillet out of the oven.

"Do you have something to put on the table to protect it from that hot pan?"

"Last drawer," he said. "Some square pads."

She put them out. "There."

"Thanks." He set down the cast-iron skillet. "There's fresh fruit salad, too."

"I'll get it." She opened the refrigerator and then bent at the waist to retrieve the bowl.

He had a perfect view of her championship-quality butt and a stirring memory of cupping it in his hands to lift her onto the table in The Pub. In spite of the cosmic joke that was his life, he went hot all over, but most of the blood traveled south of his belt. Fortunately she didn't look at him when she closed the refrigerator door. She just headed to the table with the fruit bowl.

"Do you want coffee?" he asked.

"No, thanks. I'm not quite brave enough to risk that just yet." She glanced over her shoulder. "Can I pour you a cup?"

"Just sit. I'll get it."

He did and then joined her at the table where they would eat together again. For the first time since he'd lost his professional hockey career and his family, he felt the absence of loneliness. It seemed the darkness was no match for Tess's sunny disposition.

She took a bite of food, and almost instantly her eyes closed in ecstasy. It was so sexy, he thought there was a very real chance that his head would explode.

"This is so good," she said.

He took a bite and could barely taste it. Weird since this dish was one of his favorites. "I'm glad you like it."

"I do." Her eyes sparkled when she met his gaze. "You have skills, too."

He knew she meant cooking, but the way his body was responding to her made the words a double entendre. After a swig of hot coffee, his cynical side woke up completely and reminded him he was being the worst kind of dope. He needed to make sure his rational self stayed highly caffeinated.

"So, what's on your agenda today?" she asked.

"I plan to stop by The Pub and check on the construction progress. Then there's a pile of paperwork at the rink that I need to deal with."

"Sounds exciting."

He sipped more coffee. "What about you? This is kind of a forced vacation for you."

"I plan to inspect the destruction your contractor has done. What you so cavalierly call renovation." She held up a hand to stop his protest. "I won't stay long and Nate gave me one of those masks like the guys wear so I don't breathe in the dust."

"So he knows you're pregnant?"

"I told him, but he was too polite to ask who the father is. And I didn't volunteer the information."

He nodded, appreciating her discretion. "Still, do you think it's wise to go there? Even with the mask?"

"It will be fine. Especially since I'm seeing the doctor right after."

"Is something wrong?"

"No. Regular monthly check."

He was aware of that and also knew that during the last couple of months, the doctor visits would increase in frequency until the baby was born. But he didn't tell her he knew that, because she'd already asked a lot of questions about *how* he knew so much about pregnant women and infants. Since he was trying to forget it ever happened, he never talked about that time.

The pain of being shut out by the woman who'd deceived him never went away, and remembering just brought it all up after he'd struggled so long and hard to push it down. But he couldn't ignore the doctor's appointment for the baby that might be his.

"You weren't going to tell me about seeing the doctor today?"

"No big deal. This isn't my first visit. I didn't think you'd be interested in being there or that you cared at all about it."

"I do."

The words came out before he could adequately weigh how they would sound or what the consequences would be. The reasons he cared were complicated but that didn't mean it wasn't true.

"You're acting as if I'm pulling a fast one." She sounded irritated and he wondered if there was something she didn't want him to find out about.

"Are you?"

"Of course not. Would you like to come along?"

"Damn right I'm coming with you."

Chapter Five

Who knew Leo Wallace could cook? After an unexpectedly good breakfast, Tess went upstairs to get ready for her prenatal doctor visit. She took extra care with her makeup and hair, then added a navy blazer to her white T-shirt and jeans. If she was being honest, she was bothering with her appearance because Leo was going with her. He might think she was a lying weasel dog, but by God, she was going to be a well-groomed, attractive one.

To finish off the outfit, she stepped into three-inch wedges because Leo was really tall, and beside him she didn't want to look like a refugee from the land of the seven dwarfs. Now that she thought about it, maybe he wouldn't go in the exam room with her to meet the doctor.

That seemed unlikely, though, given his level of suspicion. She suspected this appointment, for him, was about gathering information to support his doubts about fathering her baby. How were they going to handle that?

"We have some talking to do, Leo," she said to her reflection in the bathroom mirror.

In her high shoes, she carefully walked downstairs and found him in the kitchen, leaning back against the counter, where a cup of coffee was close by. He was looking at his cell phone and glanced up when she came in the room. Actually he did a double take and that was like a blast of sugar to her carb-deprived ego. Worth it, she thought about her coiffing efforts.

"Are you ready to go?" he asked.

"Why? Do I not look put together?"

"No. You look—" He stopped and there was an approving gleam in his eyes. "Nice. Really nice."

"I guess that's marginally better than 'I thought you were going to do your makeup and hair.'"

"You always look nice," he said.

Typical guy. And she was stalling. "Look, Leo, we have to talk."

"About what?" A wary look replaced his approval.

"I don't know how to explain you." The words came tumbling out and he looked confused. Tess didn't blame him. "The thing is, I've been going to Dr. Thompson forever. I don't know what to say about you. Us. If you go into the exam room with me."

"That's the plan."

She'd expected a little squirming about breaching this totally female ritual. Maybe relief that she was giving him an out. Instead he looked ready to defend his stance. "How do I put it? '*I* know you're the father of my baby, but you have doubts about whether or not that's true.' That makes me look bad."

"Doesn't make me look too good either."

"So how do we do this? Should we tell her you're not sure about being the father?"

"You told me I am."

"Because you are. But do we share all that? Are we going to have this discussion in front of the doctor?"

"Do you want to talk about it with her?"

Her response was immediate, decisive and forceful. "Good God, no."

"Then you decide how we play this. The game plan is up to you."

"A sports metaphor?"

"It makes me happy." He shrugged. "What would make you happy?"

If it was true: that they were ecstatic about the arrival of their first child. She sighed. "Would you mind terribly pretending to be what I already know you are? The father of this baby?"

"I think I can manage that," he said.

"Okay." She nodded resolutely but was secretly relieved that he was going along with her suggestion. "Then we're going to be excited, expectant parents."

"Are you excited?" he asked.

"About pretending in front of my doctor?" The thought made her more nauseated than the smell of coffee.

"No. I meant about having a baby. Being a mom. You've never said how you feel about it."

"I wish I could say yes without reservations, but I can't."

"Why?"

"For one thing, I don't know if I'll be a very good mom. Mine wasn't, so zero role model there."

"What happened?"

Apparently her grandfather hadn't said anything to him. "When I was six, my mother left me with Granddad and never came back. Last I heard she's in Florida with some guy."

"What about your father?"

"He left her—pregnant and alone." She met his gaze. "If children learn what they live, that doesn't bode well for my being a good mother."

"I don't think there's anything to worry about."

"Easy for you to say. You're not the one giving birth."

"You're not alone." That might be a general reference to him sticking around, at least for the DNA portion of the program. "Besides, you're the most responsible person I know. And Patrick Morrow raised you to be that way."

"It seems prudent to point out that after my grandmother died, he raised my mother, too, and that didn't turn out so well. What if I take the easy way out like she did?"

"That's not who you are. The Pub is a perfect example. With profits down, it would have been easy to cut your losses and walk. But you're fighting for it."

"It's Granddad's legacy. And I love that place."

"You love your baby, too."

"I do." And that was the simple truth. "However as far as being excited, that's hard. The timing isn't good, what with trying to increase The Pub's customer base. And—" she watched him watching her "—the circumstances aren't exactly desirable, if you know what I mean."

Evidence of that was him saying "your baby," not "our baby." They had to get their act together before taking it on the road. "It's your baby, too. Our baby. In front of the doctor anyway."

"Right." He looked at the time on his phone. "We should probably get going. I'll drive."

"I can."

"We're taking my car. I don't fit in that glorified skateboard you call a car."

She looked up at him, then let her gaze linger on his wide chest and impossibly wide shoulders. The memory of being held in his strong arms was never far from her thoughts. She swallowed once and said, "I think you might be able to squeeze in but it would take the jaws of life to get you out. So you win."

"Funny." The tone was sarcastic but he grinned.

Wow, Leo was quite the handsome charmer when he

didn't scowl. Hopefully the doctor would see that man and not the one who kept reminding her he didn't trust her.

They made a quick stop at The Pub, and she was pretty vocal about the fact that tearing down walls was like ripping her heart out. So Leo hurried her back to the car and headed to the doctor's office.

The medical building was located on the west side of Huntington Hills, and Leo parked in the lot. They got out and walked to the door leading to the lobby. He opened it for her and they took the elevator to the second floor. Once inside the Women's Wellness Center, he slid his arm around her waist. It was like being on a movie set when someone yelled, "Action." He was ready to play his part, so let the pretending begin. But darn she liked him touching her.

After signing in they sat together on a love seat in the waiting room. Across from them was a very pregnant woman, and a man was rubbing her big belly and talking to it. She glanced up and saw Leo watching them, too. He didn't seem horrified. Another couple had a newborn in an infant carrier and the woman's not-yet-flat tummy was proof she'd recently given birth. Finally she noticed a toddler running around with her mom and dad in hot pursuit. They looked tired, probably from chasing their daughter around. People in various stages of having children. Being a family.

The door beside them opened and a woman in scrubs said, "Tess Morrow."

They stood and followed her, stopping at the scale in the hall. A note was made in her chart, and then they were moving again and she stopped at the bathroom, where she was instructed to leave her sample. After that Tess found the room and sat on the exam table, where her blood pressure was taken. The nurse informed them that she would be seen soon.

A few minutes later Dr. Thompson walked in and smiled. "Hi, Tess. How are you?"

"Good." She glanced at Leo who'd stood and was now beside the exam table, rubbing her back. "This is Leo Wallace, the baby's father."

"Nice to meet you. Congratulations."

"Thanks." He smiled at Tess. "I couldn't be here before, but I'm glad I could make this appointment."

"Leo and I met at The Pub," Tess said quickly. "My grandfather introduced us."

"And now you're having a baby together. It must be hard for you that Patrick isn't here. He'd be very happy for you."

Probably not, Tess thought, risking a glance at the man beside her. "Yeah."

"We couldn't be happier," he said. "It was a surprise, but definitely exciting. Can't wait to be parents."

Tess wondered if she was the only one who thought he was spreading it on a little thick.

"I told Tess but it goes for you, too," Dr. Thompson said to him. "Feel free to take any of the pamphlets on the wall there. They're full of facts and suggestions for pregnancy, links on the internet and books that I've vetted for my patients. With a lot of misinformation out there, these will save you time, effort and needless anxiety. Happy mother, happy, healthy baby."

"That's the plan." He settled his muscular arm across Tess's shoulders and gave her a hug.

"And I'm here. Anything I can do to help, just let me know. Okay, lay back on the table." The doctor put a small ultrasound device on Tess's belly and explained that it would identify the baby's heartbeat. She smiled broadly. "Sounds really good and strong."

Then she pulled a tape measure taut over Tess's abdomen to determine the baby's approximate size. "Definitely growing. Everything is normal."

"That's great." Leo was holding her hand and squeezed it before helping her to a sitting position.

The doctor frowned a little as she looked at the chart. "You've lost some weight. Are you eating right?"

"Morning sickness has been a challenge," she said. "Leo gave me crackers and that helped. But it's getting much better now."

"And I convinced her to move in with me," he added. "I'm making sure she eats."

"Good." The doctor beamed at them as if they were parental stars. "You make a beautiful couple and this is going to be one good-looking baby. I've known Tess since she was a teenager. It does my heart good to see her so happy now."

That was a leap, Tess thought, but no way she was calling the doctor on it. After all, that meant she was buying the excited, expectant parent act. Leo had pulled it off brilliantly, and that was a surprise, considering how he really felt.

Of course the doctor asked if they had any questions and Leo did. About her due date and the time frame for when she'd conceived. He did it diplomatically and unless one knew why he was asking, there was no way to tell he was anything but curious. And, gosh golly, the date of her grandfather's memorial was smack-dab center of the primary window. Tess shot him an "I told you so" look and he gave a small shrug.

They left the office and Tess was relieved that things had gone without a hitch. Leo was a really good actor and no one could tell they weren't a couple. When her next appointment rolled around, she hoped to be back in her apartment and coming here alone. And that's when she felt a hitch in her heart. A reminder that it wasn't a good idea to get sucked into the fantasy of them being a real, traditional family. It would hurt like crazy when she was by herself.

After dinner with Tess, Leo left the house and drove to the ice rink. The business was open 24/7 and he made it a point to stop by at different times to check things out. It had stopped hemorrhaging money after he had made some common-sense changes and hired a new manager who knew hockey.

Buying the rink didn't make a whole lot of investment sense, and it wasn't about ego or vanity from his player years. He loved the ice. It was a purely emotional decision, so he understood how Tess felt about The Pub.

Tess was something. Honest and straightforward. She could have said she was beyond excited about having a baby when he'd asked, but she had told him her misgivings. As she'd said, he wasn't the one giving birth, hence his body wasn't changing. But her facts were indisputable. They weren't married.

And being at the doctor's with her today brought back a lot of memories. Ones that had been good but now brought a wave of pain and emptiness that nearly sent him driving off the road. It seemed like yesterday that he and his wife were over the moon about her being pregnant. He was still playing hockey and the team had a home game, giving him a chance to be at the first appointment.

Once he'd found out he was going to be a father, he'd vowed to be better than his own. He and Nancy were going to be the best parents in the history of parenting.

But it hadn't turned out that way, and he carried the torture of that inside him every single day.

He didn't believe in silver linings, but he drew on that experience earlier. At Dr. Thompson's office he had tapped into those feelings to play the role of a man who was completely thrilled about becoming a father. The ob-gyn put the time of conception at right about when he'd been with Tess. Along with the blood test and her unshakable assertion that he was the baby's father, he was starting to believe it was true. So, what now?

He had to put off thinking about that because the ice rink was coming up on his right. He pulled into the lot and noted that there were a lot of cars, which meant business was good.

After finding a space, he parked and then went inside. Immediately the smell of cold hit him, and for a few moments there was a sensation of peace, home. When he was a kid and his parents were screaming hateful things at each other, the only sanctuary he could count on was the ice.

The area around the rink had rubber padding to protect skate blades when outside the rink itself. This time of night was a free skate, meaning no lessons or practices. Anyone could come in and rent equipment to skate around the oval. It was almost time for the session to end.

He turned away and headed to the office on the second floor. There was a big glass window that looked out over the facility, and a desk facing it. Metal filing cabinets lined the wall, along with a trophy case holding pictures and awards from winning teams sponsored by the facility. It had been a while, but he wanted to make Huntington Hills Skating Rink competitive again.

He walked inside. "Hey, Mark."

The manager turned away from the window and

smiled. Mark Reeves was in his midthirties, tall and muscular, with black hair and brown eyes. They'd been competitors in professional hockey, but off the ice were good friends. The guy didn't need the money from this job any more than Leo did, and had invested along with him. But he wanted to be involved at a grassroots level.

He stood and held out his hand. "Leo. How are you?"

"Good," he lied, taking the other man's hand in his own and shaking it. "How's our business?"

"Profits are up. Not as much as I'd like, but going in the right direction."

"That's what I want to hear." He glanced out the window and saw that the number of people was starting to thin out. "I like what I see. You've added a team to the under-sixteen age group?"

"Yeah. Community outreach is starting to pay off. Adding is good. We can't afford to lose a team."

"Yeah." Leo knew all about that. Ice time for practice had a rental fee. There was revenue from skating sessions like the one just winding down now. But all services—skating lessons, blade sharpening, the shop they'd opened for selling equipment and apparel—all of it added up. And every hour of the day, ice time had to be utilized to bring in profit.

He looked at his friend. "Is everything in place for the Sticks for Kids roller hockey event?"

Mark nodded. "I have the park permits and supplies. We'll be working on stick handling and drills to promote teamwork. Kids bring their own rollerblades."

"Good."

"I've lined up some players from the men's ice hockey team I coach to help with younger kids. Education is the cornerstone of everything. It creates buzz for the sport and hopefully interest in playing ice hockey."

"Sounds like you have everything under control."

He turned and looked out over the ice again. It was Thursday night and there were teenagers hotdogging in and out of families with younger kids. One little guy caught his eye, in between his parents and holding their hands as he walk-skated unsteadily.

If things hadn't gone to hell with his own family, he'd be doing that with Chad. Wondering how the boy was doing drove him nuts. Just then the boy in the rink fell and started to cry. His dad picked him up and brushed the ice off his pants, then comforted him. Exactly what a dad should do. The trio headed for the break in the wall around the rink and stepped off.

Dad was still holding the little boy and they headed for the exit. Probably going home for his bath, bedtime rituals and good-night hugs. Leo missed that time the most, and the small arms that had no chance of reaching around his shoulders but meant everything to him.

"Leo?"

"Hmm?" He turned away and met his friend's questioning gaze. "Sorry. I was thinking about something else. You were saying?"

"Are you going to be at the community event? People want to meet the highest-scoring defenseman who ever played."

"I'm planning on it." He rested a hip on the desk. "Every participant comes away with a free stick and ball, right? We have enough?"

"I think so. We'll use leftovers at the next clinic."

Leo nodded approval. "We might want to have that one on the other side of town."

"Sounds good."

"So, show me the new snack bar."

"We're getting positive feedback, pardon the pun." Mark grinned at his joke.

Leo groaned. "I hope the food is better than your sense of humor."

After following his friend downstairs, he noted the addition of more tables and chairs where customers could relax with a hot dog, a cup of hot chocolate or a soft drink. Soup, chili and taquitos, among other things, had been added to the menu. There was a teenage girl cleaning up and shutting it down. He'd interviewed her, but hadn't seen her in action yet.

Mark stopped at the counter. "Hey, Denise, how's it going?"

"Hi, Mr. Reeves." The pretty gray-eyed blonde looked at Leo. "Nice to see you again, Mr. Wallace."

"How's business?" She was a good hire, Leo thought. Smart, polite, pretty. Adults loved her because she was great with kids. And teenage boys would gather around her like bees to honey.

"It's really good," she said. "I was going to talk to Mr. Reeves, but since you're here, too…"

"What's up?" he asked. "Don't tell me you're quitting."

"No way." Her ponytail flipped from side to side when she shook her head. "Just the opposite. When school is out for summer, I was hoping to increase my hours. I only have one more year until I go to college, and I need to save all the money I can."

Leo looked at Mark, who gave a thumbs-up. "That would be great. We'll definitely work something out."

Possibly a rink-sponsored college scholarship, Leo thought.

"Thanks."

"So, you're closing up?" He noticed a foil-covered plate of food next to the cash register.

The teen followed his gaze, and what could only be guilt settled on her face. "It's leftovers."

Mark frowned. "No problem to take it. You'd just have to throw it out."

"It's not for me…" She stopped and, if possible, looked more guilty.

"What?" Leo nudged.

"I don't want to rat him out, but—"

"Now you have to tell us." Leo kept his voice light. He didn't want to scare her. "This business is our responsibility, and if something is going on we need to know."

"He's right, kiddo," Mark agreed.

She caught her bottom lip between her teeth. "I don't think it's against the law exactly. Maybe trespassing—"

"Why don't you let us decide," Leo said gently. Loyalty was pretty important to him but sometimes you needed to spill the whole truth. "No one has to know where the information came from. We'll keep your name out of it."

Her expressive face gave away the conflict raging inside her. Finally she nodded. "There's a boy from one of the teams. He slept here last night."

Mark looked surprised. "Whoever's working a shift is supposed to do rounds—"

It would be easy to hide, Leo realized. Men's teams rented ice time off-hours for practices and games. The place was big, with a lot of dark corners. Someone familiar with it could find a place to crash and not be noticed. And he was being fed.

Denise met his gaze, looking embarrassed and ashamed. "I know him from school, too. He's got problems at home and I felt sorry for him."

Déjà vu, Leo thought. "You did the right thing. And you're not in trouble. Just, if something like this happens again, come to us. We'll figure it out."

"Okay." She told them where to find him and gave Leo the plate of food. "His name is Josh."

Leo told Mark he would handle it, then went to the men's locker room. There was a small storage space and that's where he found Josh sleeping, using his bulky hockey bag for a pillow.

He turned on the light and the boy opened his eyes, then sat up. "Hi, Josh."

"How do you know my name?"

"I own this place. It's my business to know what goes on," he said vaguely. He handed over the plate. Teenage boys could eat more than half their weight in hamburgers and french fries, and it didn't matter whether or not the food was warm. "I thought you might be hungry."

The kid answered with a sullen, negative head movement.

"Why don't you let me call your folks? I'll even give you a ride home."

"No."

"What's your last name?"

"You own this place. I thought you knew everything."

They went back and forth for a while and he got no information. Clearly the boy didn't want to go home. Leo sympathized, but letting him sleep here was out of the question.

He decided it was time to get tougher. "You're trespassing, you know. I'll just call the cops. Let them get the information out of you."

"Go ahead," he challenged. "Anything is better than living with them."

Twenty years ago Leo was this kid. He hadn't run away from home but it had crossed his mind. What if someone had called the cops on him? There had to be a compromise. "Look, my name is Leo—"

"I know. Leo 'The Wall' Wallace. Highest-scoring defenseman in the NHL." There was a little bit of awe in his voice.

Maybe he could work that angle, Leo thought. Get Josh's trust and take him to the house. Tess was there. He liked the sound of that but hoped it had more to do with her as backup for this kid crisis than anything personal.

"What would you think about coming home with me?"

Chapter Six

Tess was sitting in the family room, idly using the TV remote to flip through channels while she waited for Leo. A part of her was really looking forward to seeing him, in a "crush on a boy" sort of way. The other part of her wanted to discuss the bar in a "what the heck are you doing to my grandfather's legacy" way. When she'd seen the demolition, her stomach had turned and it had nothing to do with morning sickness.

Oh, Leo had shown her the architectural plans and the computer images of how it was going to look, but now all she saw was an empty shell where there'd once been warmth and laughter. And maybe her imagination was working overtime, but tonight it seemed to her as if he'd been gone a lot longer than he'd led her to believe he would be.

Then she heard the front door open and angry voices drifted inside. He wasn't alone. Her first thought was that he'd taken her suggestion not to let her presence cramp his social life. That was followed by an unreasonable explosion of anger, with all the characteristics of jealousy. Seconds later it sank in that the person with him wasn't a woman. Curiosity got the better of her and she left the family room to meet him in the entryway and find out what was going on.

The heated conversation stopped when they saw her.

Leo had brought home a hostile teenage hockey player, if that oversize, smelly equipment bag was anything to go by.

She stopped in front of the newcomer, who didn't smell much better. "Hi. I'm Tess. Who are you?"

"You don't need to know," he said rudely.

"This is Josh," Leo said.

He was cute, she noted, in a purely observational way. Blond hair, green eyes, a little skinny but give him a few years and he would be a heartbreaker, just like Leo. Unlike her partner, he was anything but easygoing. Intensity rolled off this kid like sweat.

She looked at the other adult in the room. "What's going on?"

"Josh was crashing at the ice rink. Some beef with his folks. He wouldn't say what it was or give me any other information. I couldn't leave him there and the only other choice was to call the cops."

"Obviously there was another option because here you are with him," she pointed out. Her guess would be that Leo didn't want to call the authorities. That would have been easier, to let them deal with whatever was going on, but that's not what he'd done. The fact that he was getting involved gave her a sudden warm and fuzzy feeling.

"Are you hungry, Josh?"

"No." He tried to look sullen, but couldn't quite pull it off.

"It's a well-known fact that, at your age, boys are always hungry. I'll warm a plate in the microwave." She turned away. "Follow me. And leave that bag by the front door. It smells like a squirrel crawled in there and died."

Someone behind her laughed and it didn't sound like Leo. That was a start.

She knew her business partner well enough now to

know that he would have protested if he didn't approve of feeding this kid, so she led the way to the kitchen.

Tess pulled leftover baked chicken and fried potatoes, along with green beans, from the refrigerator and filled a plate before putting a cover on it. Then she put everything in the microwave and hit the warm-plate button on the panel. The light inside came on along with a low hum.

The kid was hovering in the space between the family room and kitchen island. He wasn't going to talk unless he felt comfortable and trusted them. How did they pull that off? She glanced at Leo and he looked uncertain, too. What would her grandfather have done?

Basics, she thought. "Okay, Josh no-last-name—"

"I have a last name," he muttered.

"Then let's have it," she said firmly.

"It's Hutak."

"Okay, Josh Hutak, there's a powder room down the hall. Why don't you wash up before you eat." She could see a protest forming and cut it off. "That's not optional and I recommend you don't even think about talking back. No wash, no food. Not negotiable."

Hunger must have won out because the kid turned without another word and did as requested.

When it was just her and Leo, she said, "What are we going to do with him? His parents must be worried sick."

"I would be." Something in those three words said he knew how it felt to be concerned about a child. He dragged his fingers through his hair. "I'm hoping I can get through to him and he'll voluntarily give up information. If he doesn't, that leaves no choice but to—"

"Call the police," she finished. "We could let him stay but the thought of what his parents must be going through makes me want to shake the information out of him."

"I know. But the way to a man's heart is through his

stomach, and all that. We'll keep this low-key if possible. I'd really rather not escalate the situation to that level."

Leo Wallace, heartless womanizer, was empathizing with this kid big-time, and Tess was curious. Clearly she knew nothing about this man beyond his lucrative hockey career and business pursuits, not to mention his pursuit of starlets and models. But she had a feeling there was a lot more to him than that.

The microwave beeped, indicating the food was warmed. At the same time Josh came back into the room.

"Have a seat at the table."

He did as instructed and she gave him utensils while Leo poured him a big glass of milk.

"Thanks," he mumbled before digging in.

Everything disappeared quickly, as he practically inhaled it all. She'd cooked that night and wanted to believe it was about her skills, but figured he just hadn't eaten for a while. That was concerning.

"Do you want more?" she asked.

"No."

She and Leo sat across from him at the table and waited for the kid to open up about his situation but he outstubborned them.

Finally Leo cleared his throat. "I didn't like my parents very much when I was growing up. They argued all the time. More than once, one or both of them screamed at each other that they wished they'd never gotten married. My mother and father were the poster couple for why bitterly unhappy people should not stay together and make everyone around them miserable."

"Are they still together?" Tess couldn't stop herself from asking. Where Leo was concerned, the list of questions was growing, and this seemed like the least intrusive.

"No. They split when all of us kids were out of high

school. But the damage was done. I have a brother and sister, and all three of us want no part of marriage thanks to them."

"It sucks." Josh's comment and emphatic tone indicated he was going through something similar.

Tess felt obliged to point something out. "Since we're sharing sucky family stuff, I need to tell you two it could have been worse."

"How?" Leo and Josh said together. They shared a fleeting grin.

"My father, the sperm donor, disappeared before I was born. When I was six, my mother and I came to Huntington Hills to live here with her father. She left to go to the store one day and never came back. So he raised me, but I didn't have either parent."

"You had your grandfather," Leo said.

"And he was awesome." There were times, like now, when the pain of missing him was hard to bear. "But I was different from most of the other kids at school. They all had a mom or dad, or both. No one I knew lived with a grandparent. It made me different that neither of my parents wanted me."

"I wish mine didn't," Josh muttered.

"Okay," Leo said. "I think we should declare Tess the winner of the 'worst parents ever' award. But, Josh, reading between the lines, I'm hearing that your mom and dad fight with each other but both care about you. I have a feeling you're getting flack for something. What's really going on?"

The boy stared at the empty plate in front of him, then looked up and glared. "I'm grounded from hockey."

"Why?" Leo asked.

"Because they suck."

"There's something you're not telling us." He didn't

flinch from the kid's hostile gaze. "I've been where you are. My parents didn't like each other but both of them wanted what was best for me."

"So you're saying it's my fault they fight?"

Leo's expression was bemused. "I'm not sure how you got there from what I said. No, their fights are with each other. I have a feeling they're in agreement about something that's going on with you. I can't help if you don't tell me what it is."

Tess was mesmerized by the gentle understanding in his voice. This was a side of him she had never seen before. It was a good side.

"Why did they take hockey away?" he asked.

Josh looked so achingly young and the pain on his face was tangible. There was also frustration and injustice tangled up in his expression. "I'm failing English. It's stupid. They know I want to play pro hockey someday but how can I if they won't let me be on the team now?"

"I see." Leo looked thoughtful. "So, what if you pull up that grade?"

"I'm back on the team," he grudgingly admitted. "But there's no way I can. I have to pass every quiz before the final and do an extra-credit paper on *The Great Gatsby* to pass the class. I'm just screwed."

"Maybe you could get a tutor," Tess suggested. "If your parents see that you're trying, you might be able to negotiate hockey reinstatement, pending your final grade."

"They'd never go for it."

"Well," Leo said, "running away from home isn't going to keep you on the team. It's an expensive sport."

The kid's gaze was full of desperation. "Maybe you could give me a job at the rink. I'll work for hockey expenses."

"That's an idea." Leo looked thoughtful. "But you're

underage. Without your parents' consent, I would probably be breaking a whole lot of laws."

"You don't understand—"

"I do. I went through the same thing. You've got no choice," Leo said.

"What did you do?" Josh asked.

"I got my grades up in high school. There were hockey scholarships for certain colleges, and I went after one and played while I was going to school. Eventually scouts for professional teams came looking. And I was drafted." He stopped until the kid met his gaze. "But if I'd run away from home, none of that would have been possible."

"My dad won't listen," he said hopelessly.

"I'll talk to him," Leo offered. "What have you got to lose?"

Josh shrugged his shoulders. "Nothing, I guess."

"Good call. Why don't you give me your dad's number and I'll get in touch with him."

Josh thought that over for a few moments, then nodded his agreement. Leo dialed the number and introduced himself when it was answered. From this end of the conversation Tess could tell that the man knew of Leo's superstar status.

When he hung up, he smiled at the boy. "Your dad is on the way to pick you up. Let's wait for him out front. It's going to be all right. I promise."

Josh nodded, then stood and thanked Tess for dinner. After that he followed Leo out of the room and she heard the front door open and close again.

Tess couldn't believe the man she'd just seen reasoning with a teenage boy was the same one she thought had the sensitivity of an alley cat. Now she knew why he found marriage unappealing, and who could blame him. But for reasons she didn't totally get, understanding why he was that way didn't make her feel better. Because she actually liked him and that was more dangerous than simply being physically attracted.

Leo stood outside until the car's taillights disappeared. For that kid's sake, he hoped Josh's father had listened to him. He sighed and turned away, then walked back into the house, where Tess was waiting. He was glad she was there.

She'd cleaned up the kitchen from Josh's spur-of-the-moment meal and was sitting in the family room, staring at the TV, which was currently not on.

"Hey," he said.

She glanced over her shoulder to look at him. "I guess he got picked up?"

"Yeah." He walked over and sat on the couch, careful not to get too close. Being near enough to touch her wasn't a good idea.

"You were out there for a long time."

He met her gaze. "There was a little bit of a fanboy thing going on."

"So it's not just women?" she asked sweetly.

"I'm going to pretend you didn't just say that." He wished she would let that go.

"Okay. What did you say to his father?"

"I repeated the things Josh said, and Ed—that's his dad—admitted there's stress in the marriage and it could be handled better. They're in counseling."

"Good." She thought for a moment. "Did you suggest that Josh probably needs counseling, too?"

"I just met the guy," he said wryly. "It's something I'll save for our second conversation."

"His son ran away from home," she protested. "I think that's a cry for help."

"Yeah." He looked at her, all fierce and mother lion about a kid she'd just met. Maybe her instincts were on warp drive because she was pregnant. But whatever the reason, it was damn sexy. "I think his dad understands that."

"Are you sure?"

"We talked about the home situation and that Josh is caught in the middle. And the sport he loves is the only positive in his life right now. A place where he can just be a kid on a team, trying to put a puck into the other guy's net. It's a physical game but everyone is padded up and supervised. A safe place to release all those feelings you can't do anything about."

"How do you know so much about teenage boys?" she teased.

"I was one, remember?" He grinned briefly, then recalled what his life was like when he was Josh's age. "I wasn't exaggerating when I told him how it was with my family."

"Do you want to talk about it?" she asked.

"Is that your way of telling me I need counseling?"

"I would just say it straight out if I thought so." She shrugged. "All I'm saying is that I'm happy to listen."

He didn't think much about that time anymore, because he didn't feel trapped. He was a grown man and not stuck in a bitter, angry place. That was never going to happen to him again.

"Like I said, I wasn't being dramatic about my home being like a battlefield. There was no volume control. Either they were yelling at the top of their lungs or not speaking to each other at all. The tension was suffocating."

"That must have been awful."

"I didn't say anything unless absolutely necessary, for fear of setting off another round." He rested his elbows on his knees, clasping his hands together. "One time when they were wishing they never got married, I told them I wished they hadn't either. And maybe they should get a divorce."

"Uh-oh," she said.

"Yeah. He accused me of being ungrateful. She said I was selfish."

"Do you know why they didn't split sooner?"

"I asked my dad that once." He remembered bracing himself for an outburst of anger but that hadn't happened. His father had looked sad, which was worse somehow.

"What did he say?"

Leo saw sympathy in her eyes and wasn't sure how he felt about it. The look was just south of pity. "He told me they didn't want the family to be broken up."

"Oh, Leo." She sighed. "You were already broken."

"I know." And every time they'd screamed at each other about not wanting to be married, he'd vowed not to make the same mistake they had. But he had and it had been even worse.

"Do you see them much now?" she asked.

"Occasionally. He's in Washington state and she's in Florida."

"Did they pick opposite ends of the country on purpose?"

"A case could be made." He leaned back on the couch, stretching his arm across the back. With very little effort he could touch her shoulder and badly wanted to. A classic case of damned if he did, damned if he didn't. "Ironically, individually they are both nice people. But together they're like a bad chemical reaction."

"Do you think Josh's parents are like that?" she asked.

"Hard to tell. Ed seemed like a nice, reasonable guy. Worried about his son. Relieved and grateful to find out he was okay. Thanked me over and over for taking care of him."

"About that…" There was a sparkle in her expression, a look that turned the brown in her eyes the color of warm chocolate.

Leo was so used to her look of hostility and resentment, he didn't know what to make of this. "What did I do?"

"The right thing."

"Anyone else would have done the same," he said.

"Not everyone would have brought home a troubled teenage boy, let alone gotten involved in a family conflict." There was approval in her voice, something that wasn't there much when she talked to him.

He liked it.

"I didn't exactly get involved. But I did offer a piece of advice."

"Which was?"

"Don't take hockey away from Josh."

"And?" she asked.

"Ed explained that he couldn't do nothing and watch his son fail English. There had to be consequences. And that didn't mean taking away brussels sprouts."

She smiled at that and then said, "He's right."

"I agree. But I think I convinced him to make that a last resort. Give him a chance to bring up his grade, maybe with a tutor."

She nodded enthusiastically. "Now that's a really great idea."

"It was yours and I'm glad you still like it because I volunteered you. There's no time to mess around finding one and I know you like to read."

"I love to read, but—"

"Josh agreed. He likes you, by the way, and that's important. It might not work with anyone else. Ed is on board, too."

"Look, Leo—"

"I know I should have asked, but I needed to take a shot right then." Playing hockey, he'd learned strategy and setting up for a goal. No hotdogging. But sometimes you just had to swing away. A lot of times you missed the net, but every once in a while a player got lucky and scored. "I was in the zone with both of them."

"Another sports metaphor." She shook her head. "Reading between the lines, I'm going to assume you were taking advantage of your superstar reputation."

"Taking advantage sounds so harsh. I prefer to think of it as using my charm."

"Oh, please." But she didn't look upset. "Josh is such a fan, if you said jump, he'd ask how high."

"Then isn't it lucky I'm using my powers for good?" He gave her a pleading look. "Come on, Tess. It's not for long. Just help him write a paper and study for the final. The bar is closed right now anyway while the renovation is going on. So you've got the time. What do you say? This kid is at a crossroads and could go either way. Be a force for good."

She pulled her legs up to the side and angled her body toward him, sliding her shoulder out of his reach. "Are you implying that if I don't, Josh's life will be ruined?"

"I would never do that," he said virtuously.

"Oh, pull in your wings and halo, hotshot. Next thing I know you'll be walking on water." She met his gaze. "You didn't say it in so many words, but that's what I heard."

"So, what's the verdict?"

She stared at him for several moments, then nodded. "Okay. I'll help him. When do we start?"

"Tomorrow."

Her eyes widened. "Seriously?"

"He's going to meet you here after school to study for a quiz on Friday."

"I thought you said it would just be for finals," she said, pointing an accusing finger at him.

"He needs all the points he can get."

"Well, it's a good thing you didn't spring this on me. No pressure either," she said wryly.

"It's a tough time for him, Tess."

"I know. A cry for help. How can I turn my back?" Her voice softened. "I had my issues with not having parents, but in the long run maybe I was better off than you and Josh that they weren't around."

"Maybe." Thanks to Patrick Morrow, she'd turned out great. And Pat had helped Leo through one of the worst times in his life. He owed him.

"I'm tired. It's been quite a night." She stood and looked down at him. "I just have to say that you did good tonight, Leo. You're going to be a wonderful father."

He didn't say anything, just watched her leave as a too-familiar feeling of emptiness came over him. He'd been a good father once, until the kid he thought was his was ripped out of his life. That wasn't going to happen again. Not if Tess was carrying his baby.

Chapter Seven

Leo looked around The Pub and nodded with satisfaction. Plastic covers protected the booths, tables and bar. The changes were in the adjacent areas, and knocking out the wall had really opened up the place, made it brighter. In his gut he felt this was a good move and he really hoped Tess agreed. She was going to be here any minute and he was a little nervous about her reaction. The last time she saw it there was a devastated look on her face, and he couldn't make her feel better until the place was put back together. It wasn't yet. Still a work in progress.

This business wasn't just how she made her living; it was part of her history, and he'd come on pretty strong about modernizing. Doing nothing meant a slow, painful decline and eventual failure. It was the right thing to make sure this place was around for a long time to come.

The door opened behind him, and she walked in, looking so fresh and pretty, he wanted to just stare. It was a stupid reaction. He'd seen her a few hours ago at breakfast, when he realized he very much liked seeing her in the morning. And that was stupid, too. This living arrangement was temporary. And that's all it could be. He knew from personal experience not to get used to being happy, because the good stuff didn't last.

Tess was looking around and finally met his gaze. "Hi. So, it's still torn up."

"You're late." *Way to get her on your side, Wallace.*

"Sorry. I had to drop Josh off at home."

"How is the tutoring going?" Leo knew she'd been working with him twice a week for a few weeks now.

"He's a bright kid. He just doesn't like reading and writing." She shrugged. "We went through books on his suggested-reading list and I tried to steer him to one that might interest him. We're both going to read it so I can help him organize his thoughts to write the paper."

"Is he cooperative?"

"Very." She smiled. "He's polite and really funny. I enjoy tutoring him."

"Good." At least his idea for her to tutor had worked out. On the other hand, time would tell how the changes here would be. He glanced around. "So, what do you think?"

She walked around, studying the adjacent area in its rough stages. "With the wall gone, the bar will actually be in the middle of the room."

"Yeah."

"It's very open."

"Nate's guys are repairing wall board that was tweaked when the demolition was done. That takes the longest. Then there's paint."

"And when the fumes are gone, I'll be out of your hair," she said.

"You've really been a pain in the neck," he teased. The thought of her gone didn't thrill him, though.

"Speaking of finishing touches, I brought paint chips and some other decorating samples. We need window coverings and furniture."

"Let's see what you have."

She walked back into the old part and set her purse on a plastic-covered table, then pulled out paint charts in varying shades of beige, yellow, blue and green. Leo moved close to look at the colors, and their arms brushed. His gut clenched and tightened. The scent of her skin burrowed inside him and shorted out brain function until he couldn't tell the difference between gold and meadow green.

"I think we should go with earth tones," she said.

The card she held out had about six shades that went from nearly white to chocolate brown. And they all had names. He picked up another card with shades of blue.

"How about one of these?" He looked more closely. "The cerulean is eye-catching."

"Seriously?" The fact that her lips were curving up was a clue she didn't mean that in a bad way. "Hearing the word *cerulean* come out of your mouth just seems wrong somehow."

"I'm just reading the name." He pointed to it. "Seems to me this color will work with chrome and glass."

"Seriously?" This time she didn't smile.

"What?"

"Chrome and glass are only good if you want to get fingerprints at a crime scene." She held up a hand to stop his rebuttal. "Think about the time it will take to maintain. Not to mention it will completely alter the vibe. Goodbye, homey and cozy. Hello, dystopian society."

"Well, when Big Brother is watching, I hope it's here, with a game on one of our TVs."

"I'm serious," she said.

"Me, too."

"We have a core clientele that likes to come here and relax. I feel an obligation to them and their expectations. Plus we can't afford to alienate any segment of our customer base. It's like interviewing for a job. You have a small window of time to make an impression. Whether it's good or bad depends on appearance."

While listening to her passionate defense, Leo was more than a little preoccupied with her appearance. Her mouth, for one thing. He knew how good she tasted. And her hair. It was shiny and dark and pulled into a ponytail, with wisps curling around her face. She was wearing jeans that were getting tight, showing the baby bump where her stomach used to be flat. This wasn't the first time he'd noted pregnancy changes in a woman carrying his baby—at least he'd thought it was his.

"Are you listening to me?" Tess asked, breaking into his thoughts.

"Yes." Technically that was true, although he didn't really know what she'd said. Except she generally disapproved of his decorating suggestions. "Okay, how about a compromise? We continue the wood floor all the way through. Put in comfortable chairs with glass tables, a lounge feel for watching the game, as if you were in your own family room. Use earth tones in the original bar area and paint the new part a coordinating color of cerulean."

It was obvious that she didn't want to smile, but her lips twitched. When she answered, her tone was grudging. "That might work."

"Look at us. I think we just negotiated a peaceful settlement."

"It appears we have."

He grinned but it quickly disappeared. There was something else that he needed to bring up, and she was going to like it a lot less than chrome and glass.

"Tess, one more thing—"

Her expression turned wary. "Your tone isn't reassuring. You should work on that."

"Okay. But first we need to think about a new name for this place."

"What's wrong with the old one?"

"It sounds like it was made up by a man."

"It was. My grandfather." Her mouth trembled and she looked horrified when big, fat tears rolled down her cheeks. She covered her face with her hands and turned away from him. But her shoulders were shaking with silent sobs.

Leo couldn't stand seeing Tess cry now any more than the last time, right here in this room on the night of her grandfather's memorial. He put his hands on her shoulders and turned her, pulling her against his chest, then wrapping his arms around her.

"Hush. Don't cry." He patted her back.

"Damn hormones."

"It's going to work out. You'll see." That was something you said when the jury was out deliberating and you had no idea what the heck was going to happen. It was lame and all he had.

But damn, she felt good. If it made him a bastard for finding the silver lining of her distress, then so be it. Because he couldn't help the feeling. She felt even better than that night when they'd ended up having sex just a few feet from where they were standing right now. And he wanted her again. Even more than he had then.

When she abruptly pulled away from him, he was afraid he'd said that out loud. But probably not, since talking required air and suddenly it was hard for him to breathe.

Tess's hand was shaking when she brushed moisture from beneath her eyes. She drew in a deep breath, evidence that she wasn't unaffected by his touch.

"Sorry. I didn't mean to blubber."

"It's okay. I kind of surprised you by suggesting a name change. My bad."

"Would you mind if we take that up another time? I'm meeting my friends for dinner."

"No problem."

"We need to make final decisions on the finishing touches and it occurs to me that it might help to consult an interior designer. One of the regulars does that so I'll contact her and make an appointment. Let's coordinate our schedules so we can both be here."

When she pulled out her cell phone, Leo did, too. She started talking dates and he zeroed in on the current one. Between the bar renovations, the baby and thinking about Tess, he hadn't been paying attention to what day it was. But now the significance of this one sank in, making him feel as if he'd been bodychecked without hockey pads.

And for some reason, this year the pain of remembering was worse than ever.

When she walked into the restaurant called Burgers but Better, Tess was still quivering from feeling Leo's arms around her again. In the same room where they'd had sex. It would have been so easy to go there for a second time, because she wanted him. There was no denying the attraction, but acting on it would have been stupid. Once was a foolish mistake, but twice was a pattern and that was a template for heartbreak. They'd agreed not to mix business and pleasure, and she was sticking to that. Her priority was having her baby and saving her business, in that order.

And now she was going to put all that aside and have a carefree evening with her two BFFs. Tess had known Carla Kellerman and Jamie Webber since first grade. She'd come to live with her grandfather, and then her mom had split just before she started a brand-new school and knew no one. A terrified first grader had walked into the classroom and come out with two lifelong friends.

They'd been through a lot together—breakups with boyfriends, job changes, family problems and loss. There was no one she counted on more than these two women. It had been a while since she'd seen them, and since then Tess had gone through a lot of changes, life-altering ones. With The Pub closed because of the construction work, they were meeting somewhere different for dinner.

Tess got there first, which never happened because she normally got hung up at work, even before her grandfather died. But she wasn't currently working, unless tutoring counted, so that wasn't a problem. She was sitting at a booth in the brightly lit, casual restaurant when her friends walked in together and looked around.

She stood, waved and they came over. There were big hugs all around before the two of them slid into the space across from her in the booth. They smiled at each other for several moments, just happy to be together.

"The triumvirate of trouble together again." Jamie Webber was a pretty, blue-eyed brunette who labeled her hair mousey brown and her legs too short.

"That's what Granddad always called us. The last time we were together was at the memorial service." The pain of loss sliced through her. That was a sad day but she had a feeling what she would remember most was what happened between her and Leo. It was the day a life lost had been honored and another had been created.

"I miss him, too." Carla squeezed her hand for a moment. The redhead had a fiery temper and the biggest heart in the world. "A lot has changed for you since then. You're pregnant."

"Thanks for the newsflash." She'd told them about the baby, how it happened and who the father was.

"How are you feeling?" Jamie asked.

"Tired. Nauseated and generally in a state of doubt and fear. How are you guys?"

"Things are good," Jamie said. "I finally told Karl he was never getting out of the friend zone."

"How did he take it?" Both Tess and Carla had recommended letting the poor guy know sooner rather than later.

"I felt like I kicked a puppy. It was awful. You both know how I hate hurting anyone."

"We do," Carla confirmed. "And you're a brave little soldier. But letting it go on would have hurt him more in the long run. You did the right thing."

"I know." Jamie sighed, then looked sideways at Carla. "And what's going on with you?"

Tess pushed Leo out of her mind and focused on her friend. "Lots of changes, I hear. You're back home, where you belong, and have a new job."

"It's humiliating," Carla said. "Not the job. But leaving town. I can't believe I followed a guy to Denver, worked my ass off to help him get established, buy a house and then he dumped me. So now I'm back, forced to live with my mother in the house where I grew up. Full circle sucks."

"I'm sorry, honey," Tess said. "But selfishly, I'm glad you're back."

"Tell us about the job," Jamie urged.

"It's called Make Me a Match, as in matchmaking."

"So you're working at a place that brings couples together," Tess clarified.

"The irony is huge," Carla admitted. "I'm not the only one getting back on my feet. The company provides personal service and has been going through a rough patch.

The owner's nephew is some tech guy and agreed to help out for a limited time, make things run more efficiently."

"Sounds exciting," Jamie said.

"You should give us a try," Carla told Jamie.

"Actually I met someone. He's the reason I had to tell Karl how I felt. His name is Bill Para and he's in sales. Right now he's going back and forth between here and Seattle, but he's planning to move here. He says the weather is better in California."

"Can't argue with that," Tess agreed.

The waitress interrupted them and introduced herself, then took drink and food orders. It was—surprise—burgers all around. She pointed out the fixings bar that offered a plethora of items to make the hamburgers more exciting. Hence the name—Burgers but Better.

Drinks came quickly—wine for her two friends, club soda with lime for Tess. They clinked glasses.

"To the baby," Carla toasted. "I can't believe you're going to be a mother."

"Tell me about it."

Jamie turned serious. "I want to hear about this baby's father. Leo Wallace. I saw him at the memorial service and he seemed genuinely fond of your grandfather. What's he like?"

"Besides huge and hunky." Carla grinned.

"He's now my partner in the business for one thing." Tess knew that's not what they wanted to know but this was the simplest part of their relationship, and even that was complicated. "Apparently Granddad was fond of him. About six months before he died, he approached Leo about buying into the business."

"Knowing him, Pat wanted to make sure there was someone to watch over you after he was gone," Jamie said.

Tess nodded and explained about customer decline

and her reasons for going through with the partnership proposal.

"How does Leo feel about becoming a father?" Carla asked.

"That's a good question. He wants a DNA test after the baby is born. He made that very clear."

"Can't say I blame him," Jamie teased. "What with the way you sleep around. I'm surprised you could narrow it down to one guy."

"Funny girl." Tess was aware that her friends knew he was the one and only guy she'd been with in a very long time. They told each other everything. The only information she'd held back was her current living arrangement, and she wasn't sure why. But in a few weeks she'd be back in her apartment anyway. No harm, no foul. Getting serious again, she said, "He asked how I feel about being a mother."

"Wow, a man in touch with his softer side." Carla looked at Jamie and the two friends nodded at each other. "And?"

"I was honest with him. I'm nervous. It's a big change, not to mention responsibility. And I have a business to run, onc that needs to grow to be successful. That means more hours at work, not less."

"Good thing you have a partner, then," Jamie said. "Is he excited about being a dad? Maybe having a new little hockey player?"

"Honestly, I haven't actually asked him how he feels about it."

"Because you don't want to know." Carla wasn't asking.

These two knew her better than anyone and would know if she was dodging the question. So she didn't.

"That's probably true. But it's a little freaky what he knows about pregnant women."

"Oh?"

"He brought me crackers when I was having trouble keeping food down." And he'd held her hair back when she threw up. "He insisted on coming to my OB appointment." But it seemed more as if he was keeping her under surveillance than anything else. "But he has a reputation with women, so—"

"So a sports guy who's a womanizer is a deal breaker for you," Jamie said.

According to Granddad, her father was the quarterback and captain of his high school football team, and he'd run out on his family. Tess's college love was a baseball player and he'd cheated on her. In Tess's eyes, athletes didn't make good husband material. She had to keep reminding herself there would never be anything, except this baby, between her and Leo.

The waitress arrived with their burgers and fries, and they took them to the bar for bacon, jalapeno, onions and just about any topping one could imagine. After returning to the table, there was nothing but silence because their mouths were too busy eating. It was a messy meal that required concentration and a bazillion napkins. Tess didn't complain because she was happy to no longer be in the spotlight, fielding questions she couldn't answer.

"That was super yummy," Carla said when she was finished.

"I'm a happy girl," Jamie agreed. "Tess, you're lagging."

All eyes were on her half-eaten hamburger. "My appetite isn't quite back to normal yet. I'll get a to-go box. Leo might like it."

"Oh? And why is it that he would be getting your leftovers?" Jamie asked, eyes narrowing suspiciously.

"What are you not telling us?" Carla demanded.

Tess had only said there were renovations going on at The Pub. Neither of them had asked if she was staying in her apartment while the work was being done. Now she had no choice. The cat was out of the bag and no way would they let this slide.

"I had to move out because of the dust and paint fumes. Not good for the baby."

"And what does this have to do with Leo?"

Tess looked at Carla. "He was actually the one who said it wasn't a good idea for me to be there. And that his house has lots of room."

"You could have asked me," Carla said.

"Or me." Jamie wore her heart on her sleeve, and clearly her feelings were hurt.

"Oh, honey." Tess reached across the table and squeezed her hand. "I couldn't impose on you in your studio apartment. There's not enough room." She looked at Carla. "And I couldn't ask you."

"Because I'm living with my mom. But you know we could make room."

"I didn't want to inconvenience anyone. Besides, Leo was pretty insistent." She held up her hand to stop the questions she knew they still had. "Separate bedrooms. That one time was, well, one time. A mistake. We're handling the consequences together."

"How very grown-up and civilized of you both." Carla's voice was wry.

"Okay." Jamie nodded. "As long as you know we're there for you. There's no favor you can't ask. Nothing we wouldn't do for you."

"Including hurting that big hunk if he hurts you," Carla

said fiercely. "Just so you know, I can be a father if he decides it's not for him."

"Sweet of you." Tess grinned. "But anatomically you don't have the equipment to be a dad."

"Still," she said, "I've got your back. Discipline is my middle name. I can be the bad cop."

"Me, too," Jamie chimed in.

"And I love you guys for that." Tess's vision blurred with tears. "Damn hormones."

"Oh, sweetie—"

They both reached over and took her hands. She sniffled and held on tightly. There was no doubt in her mind these loyal women would be there for her.

But Leo had surprised her. He had clearly connected with Josh and handled that situation extremely well. His fathering instincts were on full display and, in her opinion, he was going to be a terrific dad. He was also anti-marriage, flat out said as much because of his folks, but she was, too. They saw eye to eye on that.

It was just the business they seemed to butt heads on. "Thanks, you guys, for being my friends. I love our girls' nights."

"Me, too." Jamie squeezed her hand tight, then let go. She looked around the restaurant. "I sure do miss the bar, though. It's so friendly and comfortable there."

"Not for much longer." Tess thought about the meeting with Leo just a couple of hours ago. The one where she brought up wanting cozy and he pushed for flashy. She had a partner now and compromises had to be made. And more darn changes.

"What do you mean not for much longer?" Carla asked the question, but both women were giving her a skeptical look.

"The decor is changing—a mix of old and new. He wants it to be a sports bar. Do you believe that?"

"Guys like sports bars," Jamie mused.

Carla nodded thoughtfully. "Could be a good place to meet men. A fun place to suggest a first get-together for our Make Me a Match clients. So right there you've added another customer demographic. Women who want to meet men."

"Oh, brother." Tess already met a man and it was complicating the stuffing out of her life.

She'd be better off alone, but… Leo gave really good hugs. When he put those big, strong arms around a girl, she knew she'd been *hugged*. It made her feel better earlier, when she had cried.

But then it made her want sex. It made her not so sure mixing business with pleasure was such a bad idea. The more time she spent with Leo, the more she was leaning toward that very bad idea.

And now she had to go back to his place and see him.

Chapter Eight

Through his alcohol-induced haze, Leo was aware of someone shaking him awake. He opened one eye and decided it must be Tess, although she was really blurry, which was a shame because he liked looking at her. She was pretty. And his head was pounding, like a bunch of midgets were bouncing on a trampoline in his brain.

He focused a little and saw she was staring at him. "What?"

She held up a nearly empty bottle of scotch. "Did you drink all this?"

He struggled to remember, and then it came back to him why he'd deliberately gotten blind drunk in the first place. Holding out his hand he said, "Shame to waste that."

"I think you've had enough."

"Not even close."

She handed him a bottle of water instead. "Alcohol is dehydrating. You need to drink this. I learned a lot of useful stuff working in The Pub."

He sat up and the room started spinning, so he leaned against the back of the sofa again and rubbed the ice-cold water bottle across his forehead. The scotch would have been gone if she'd given him that instead. Anything to achieve a reprieve from the aching emptiness of loss. Just for this day. He wasn't entitled to much but surely it was okay to make the pain go away for today.

Tess sat on the coffee table right in front of him and set the liquor bottle behind her. He'd have to go through her to get the booze. As pleasant as that thought was, he couldn't do it and at the moment wasn't entirely clear on why.

"Have you eaten?" she asked.

He shook his head and, man, was he sorry. Pain exploded inside his skull and he winced. "Not hungry."

"Could you choke down some eggs and toast? Something light. It would make you feel better."

That's just it. He would never feel better. Not about this. "No. Just go to bed. I'm pretty bad company."

"So this isn't a good-natured bender you've got going on." She met his gaze. "I've seen a lot. I know the difference. If you were in my place, I'd be taking your car keys and calling an Uber."

"I'm not planning to drive."

He opened the plastic bottle and took a long drink of water. It helped some. But he still didn't want company. Conversation was the last thing he was looking for but she didn't budge. She had a look on her face, the one women get when they're determined to drag something out of a guy. And she didn't say a word. Another tactic to get him to open up.

"I'm not going to talk," he said stubbornly.

"Okay." But she continued to look at him.

Even in his semi-sober state he could tell this silence was getting awkward. He glared at her. "What is it going to take to get you to go away?"

"Tell me about Chad."

Hearing the name was like a two-by-four to the midsection. If her goal was to sober him up with an agonizing adrenaline rush, score one for her. And then something crept into his foggy mind.

"How do you know about him?"

"I don't. But you were mumbling the name and it sounded like a nightmare. You were pretty upset. That's why I woke you. Otherwise I'd have let you sleep it off."

"You should have."

"I couldn't." Her eyes took on a softness when she said, "Tell me. Who is Chad and why are you so upset about him?"

"Is there anything I can do to make you let this go?"

"Not even giving up chrome-and-glass decor for the bar."

Any other time he would have smiled at that, but not today. "It's Chad's fourth birthday."

"And you're not there. Is that your nephew? Godson?"

"He was my son. At least I thought so." He sat forward and rested his elbows on his knees.

"I don't understand."

He needed to start at the beginning, spit out the story and never speak of it again. "A woman I was seeing told me she was pregnant with my child. I wanted to do the right thing and asked her to marry me."

"Even though you saw your parents make each other miserable."

"Yeah. I thought it would be different for me. And it was." He met her gaze. "Just not how I expected. It was so much worse."

"What happened, Leo?"

"I supported her through the pregnancy. Made sure she scheduled all her doctor appointments when I didn't have a road trip, so I could be there."

"That's how you know so much about morning sickness and pregnancy."

"Yeah."

"Sorry. Didn't mean to interrupt. Go on," she urged.

"It was a textbook pregnancy and birth. I was there when Chad was born and over the moon in love with that baby boy. My son. I was a hands-on dad. Changed diapers, did nighttime feedings. Walked the floor with him when he was teething. I did all of it and loved everything. I was a good dad. Even Nancy—"

"Who?"

"My wife—ex-wife. She used to joke that I was a better mother than her." He sighed. "When I had to be away for road games, I missed him like crazy. Worried that he was all right. Hated that I might not hear his first word, see him take his first steps. All the milestones I wanted to be there for."

Leo remembered holding that tiny body right after he was born. He couldn't even put into words the power of the feelings that had rocked him to the core. Love, protectiveness, wanting to teach him everything. He was privileged to shape a little life and be a better dad than he'd had growing up.

"You said you *thought* he was your son. He's not?"

"For two and a half years I believed he was my child. She let me fall more in love with him every day." He met her gaze and wasn't sure why the pity in hers made him angrier. "When I broke my ankle in a Stanley Cup playoff game, I was almost happy. It ended my career but that meant I didn't have to be away from my son. I'd get an act two making a living but I'd never get back the moments in his life I missed."

"How did you find out he's not yours?"

"She told me."

"What?" Tess looked shocked. "Why after all that time would she?"

He shook his head. "She was leaving me because she

was having an affair. Seeing the guy when I was on the road, playing hockey. That was bad enough, but she admitted he was Chad's biological father. They were broken up and we were dating when she found out she was pregnant. I was the rebound guy who proposed faster than the speed of light and who made pretty good money in pro hockey. She knew she'd be well taken care of. Finally she told me the truth, said she had to be honest."

"Took her long enough. Two and a half years? The lying bitch." Tess was furious.

Somehow that made him feel a little better and he smiled at her fierceness. But it was gone in a heartbeat. "I couldn't stop her leaving and taking Chad with her. But she couldn't stop me loving him."

"What happened?"

"I hired an attorney and tried to get visitation with him. The problem is, I don't share his DNA so I have no legal rights at all. She took it one step further and got the court to order me to stay away from him."

"Oh, God, Leo. So you got the double whammy—your career was over and your family was gone." She moved to the sofa and sat close enough to put her arms around him. "And today is his birthday."

"A yearly reminder that I lost everything."

"I don't know how you survived that."

"Not well. It may come as a surprise to you, but this isn't the first time I've been drunk over what happened." The effects of the scotch were wearing off but the feel of her holding him was taking over for the liquor. "Your grandfather was the one who pulled me out of it."

She looked at him. "Really?"

"I lost myself for a while but he talked me back." He smiled a little, remembering Pat teasing him about getting a plaque with Leo's name on it for the chair he always sat in. "I was a regular. And it was like a therapy session. I talked about my problems and he told me how he felt about his daughter abandoning her child."

"It couldn't have been easy for him. Becoming responsible for a six-year-old girl." She looked a little guilty about it.

"What happened wasn't your fault, Tess."

"I know, but—"

"Hey, don't go there. I've got dibs on being the star of this pity party."

"Okay." She didn't look convinced.

"For what it's worth, he told me that raising you, having you in his life, was the best thing that ever happened."

"He was just saying that."

Leo shook his head. Still a big mistake. "No. He said you kept him young and he loved you so much. He told me he was sad for his daughter, your mom, because she was missing the joy of watching you grow up. To him, you were a gift."

"Sounds like him." She smiled a little, gave him a quick hug and then slid away. "He was a good man."

"The best."

"And so are you," she insisted.

"I don't think I'm even in his league." Leo missed her warmth. Missed it too much. "I'm not sure I would have gotten through all that without him."

"Fortunately you didn't have to. It's good he was there for you when you needed someone."

He'd needed someone tonight, too, and she was there. Just like her grandfather. Well, not exactly. Pat had never hugged him. But there was something in the Morrow DNA that was good and caring. He wasn't sure he'd have gotten through this painful anniversary without her. And that bothered him more than a little. He didn't want to need anyone.

* * *

The next morning Tess was awake early, or maybe she hadn't slept much. It was impossible to get out of her mind the complete misery on Leo's face from the sad anniversary he'd told her about. She was still trying to process what he'd gone through. Not in a million years did she think she'd feel sorry for cocky, confident Leo Wallace, but there was no way not to.

That witch had used him, then basically said, "Just kidding, you really have no right to love this child after all. It's time to stop now."

That was selfish and cruel, and he didn't deserve it. He'd done what he thought was right and married her, against his better judgment and negative feelings about tying the knot.

He hadn't offered to marry Tess and she actually *was* carrying his baby. Not that she wanted to get married but still… In his shoes, she would do the same thing—wait for conclusive DNA before becoming emotionally involved with the baby.

Speaking of shoes, she heard him coming down the stairs. A man as big as him just couldn't move silently like a cat burglar. He walked into the kitchen and his hair was still damp from a shower. His eyes were bloodshot and he hadn't shaved this morning. The stubble was pretty darn sexy and he looked a little dangerous. If anything it added to his appeal, and her heart skipped a beat.

"Morning," she said. "How do you feel?"

He winced and sat on one of the barstools lined up at the granite-covered island. "Is it necessary to shout?"

"Sorry."

"It's okay."

"Do you want coffee?" she practically whispered.

"Yes."

"Are you hungry?" She gave him a sympathetic look. "I got wasted in college just once. Now that I think about it, the next day was a lot like having morning sickness. Do you feel like eating?"

He held out his hand and rocked it back and forth. "Probably just coffee."

"I know what you need." She opened the pantry and got out a box, then set it in front of him.

He pulled out one of the packages of square soda crackers and gave her a wry look. "You probably think this is funny."

"No. And this is not a joke. It might help. Just sit tight. I've got you covered." She brought him coffee and a sports drink, since he always kept some in the refrigerator. Beside that she put two Tylenol on the counter. "Your electrolytes are out of whack, so this will help replenish them and flush the impurities out of your system. The crackers are bland and will go down easily."

"Okay." He took a square and bit into it with very little enthusiasm.

"I'll make you some eggs and toast, too. You need something light. Get calories into your body to reset your system."

While talking she quickly prepared some food and set a plate in front of him, then walked around the island and sat on the stool next to his. She watched him pick at the eggs and eat a triangle of the toast she'd cut diagonally. It must have helped because after that his plate was empty pretty fast. Now he was working on the sports drink.

"Can I get you more toast? Eggs?" she asked.

He shook his head and winced a little. "No, thanks. Maybe in a little while. Need to see how that settles first."

"Okay."

He studied her through narrowed eyes that were a little

less bloodshot. "Why are you being so nice to me? Obviously you don't approve of my dating style. I thought you'd be gloating. Thinking I got exactly what was coming to me. Poetic justice."

"So you do remember telling me about it." She hadn't been sure, although he'd been pretty articulate. Even with his voice slurred by the scotch. The day after a bender some people had no recollection of what they'd said. "I wasn't sure you did."

"Yeah, I remember." The dark look he'd worn last night was back.

"I can't believe you assume I'm the kind of person who would think what that woman did to you was okay under any circumstances. She lied to you and her child. That little boy thought you were his father. He bonded with you. And you with him." She shook her head at the injustice, disgusted by the deception. "There's no excuse for what she did. How confused that child must have been."

"Yeah. It wasn't a hallelujah moment for me either."

"Of course not. At least on some level you understood what was happening. But he was young. That's a blessing in a way. He probably won't remember." She stared at him. "There's less chance of that awful situation messing him up."

"Can't say the same for me. I remember it all." He wasn't drunk now, but the bitter, angry expression was still there in his eyes, on his face.

"What she did was despicable. Unconscionable. She deceived you in the cruelest possible way. On top of that she cheated on you…" Tess was momentarily at a loss for words that were bad enough to describe what happened to him. "I honestly don't understand how she could do something like that."

One of his eyebrows arched. "I was gullible. A sap. A fool."

"No." She was adamant. "Did you make the decision to date a woman who was a liar? If the answer to that question is no, which I'm sure it is, why in the world would you question whether or not you were the father of her baby?"

"I had no clue she wouldn't know the truth if it walked up and shook her hand."

"Then you're not a fool."

He looked surprised. "Don't look now but I think you just defended my honor."

"Guess I did." And didn't she feel just the tiniest bit sheepish and guilty. "I can see based on our recent history why it would come as a shock."

"Just a little."

"Well, brace yourself for another one. I understand why you're so determined to have a DNA test done when the baby is born. After going through that awful experience, I can't blame you at all."

"If that had never happened to me…" He cradled the mug of black coffee between his big hands and then met her gaze. "But it did, and here I am again. Trust is hard."

"I know." She nodded emphatically. "And we'll have to wait for proof. But for what it's worth, I can assure you that before my grandfather's memorial, I hadn't slept with anyone for a really long time. Over a year. Probably more. It's been so long, I can't even remember when I last had sex…"

Tess realized what she was saying, the intimate information she was revealing, and felt her cheeks burn with embarrassment. If only the earth would open up and swallow her right this minute. She couldn't even look at him.

"You're blushing," he pointed out.

"Thanks for stating the obvious."

"It's cute."

"Not if you're me. I don't suppose you'd like to share how long it had been since you'd had sex, before that night?" She met his gaze but he didn't respond. He simply looked amused. "I didn't think so. But I bet the women you go out with don't blush."

"So, we're back to that. I'm sorry you think so little of me." He sighed. "Full disclosure. Most of them are using me."

"Like Nancy?" Tess's gaze lifted to his. "And you're okay with that?"

"Not like her. No one is lying. Everyone's motives are right out on the table. They're mostly models and actresses looking for publicity to further their careers. I'm a bachelor who used to be in sports. I do endorsements, and a lot of people know who I am. When I'm photographed with a woman on my arm, the rumors and gossip go crazy. Inquiring minds want to know if this is the one who finally caught Leo Wallace. It gets her name out there. When they need a public-relations shot of adrenaline, the publicist calls with a heads-up that I'm 'dumping' them."

"And you're okay with being the bad guy?" she asked.

"Sure." He shrugged. "They always say nice things about me. Bottom line is that there's never anything serious. No one is hurt; no broken hearts. It's just words and if someone's career gets a bump out of it, I'm good with that."

Tess felt petty and small. "That's actually really nice of you."

"I keep telling you I'm a sweetheart of a guy."

Obviously her grandfather thought so or he wouldn't have wanted him to buy into the business and be her partner. Now Tess felt kind of awful. She'd been downright unfriendly to him based on what she'd read about him in magazines. In reality he was doing those women a favor. Since their guards were down at the moment, this might be a good time to explain her hostility.

"I was wrong about you." She met his gaze. "You may have noticed that my attitude toward you was a little cool."

"Really? That was you? I thought we were on the brink of another ice age." For the first time since he'd walked into the kitchen, there was a twinkle in his eyes.

It might be that he was feeling relief at unburdening himself. Or he was enjoying the prospect of her eating crow. Or both. Either way she was glad he seemed to be snapping out of the despondent mood of last night. If she had to grovel a little, that was okay with her. But it was important that he understand why she'd jumped to conclusions about him.

"In college I had a boyfriend."

"Only one? I would think a girl as pretty as you would have guys lined up."

The compliment made her feel warm and gooey inside, and then the painful memories threw a bucket of ice water on her amusement.

"There was a line all right, but not for me. He was an athlete, a star, and women couldn't seem to help throwing themselves at him."

"I'm guessing he didn't throw them back." His eyebrows drew together in a frown.

"I thought he did. At first. Then I caught him cheating and confronted him."

"So you cut him loose," he guessed.

"Not then. I gave him a second chance. And a third. Each time he told me it wouldn't happen again. He loved me and begged me to forgive him. I was in love so I believed him." She looked up and wondered what the expression in his eyes meant. "So I'm the gullible one. The sap. The fool who was drawn to the aura of the athlete and got squeezed out in the crush of adoring women."

"That explains why the first time we met you gave me a look that could laser the paint off a car."

It was her turn to wince. "I apologize for that. It was very unfair of me."

"Don't worry about it. Now I understand why. Guess we both have baggage." He put his big hand over hers. "But I want you to know that not all athletes are jackasses."

"Point taken," she said. "And not all women are lying bitches."

"Understood."

His warm hand felt so good holding hers. Every time he touched her, she felt breathless and weak in the knees. Sometimes he didn't even have to touch her. One look could render her tongue-tied and out of breath. In fact the look he was giving her right now, a combination of teasing and tender, was making her want to crawl into his lap and put her arms around him. That made it so much harder to say what she had to because it couldn't happen.

"We do have baggage," she repeated. "Trust is hard for me, too. My biological father abandoned my mother. Then she left me, too. And I took a chance anyway and ended up getting hurt. And you've made it clear you don't want a commitment." She slid her hand out from underneath his. "Clearly neither one of us wants to get personally involved."

"I couldn't agree more," he said. "Our partnership is business, not pleasure."

"Exactly." She nodded and smiled. "And when the baby is born and the DNA is done, we'll work out a parenting agreement fair to both of us."

"That sounds good."

It didn't feel good to her, though. They were staking out positions to clarify there would be nothing romantic between them. They were flat out saying that trust was an issue. Except that after what he told her about his past, Tess wasn't simply attracted to a handsome, sexy man. She found out he was someone she could like and really respect. How odd that she felt closer to him.

And still so very far away.

Chapter Nine

Josh was at the house for his tutoring session. The two of them were sitting at the kitchen table, and she was keeping him company while he took a mock quiz in preparation for his last exam on the Shakespeare play *Romeo and Juliet*. Leo was out doing whatever it was he did all day. Business stuff that kept him busy until dinnertime. She'd thought he worked a lot in his home office, but not since she moved in here. Was he avoiding her? It was a riddle for another time, and she wouldn't let the answer matter one way or the other.

Tess had talked to Josh's teacher and looked through previous tests to come up with study points for him to work on. While the kid agonized over literature, she brooded over Leo Wallace. It had been a week since his shocking revelation about his past. Seven days and nights spent under his roof while she looked at him in a completely different way.

He was a man who deeply loved a little boy he'd thought was his. Now he was under court order not to see this child and she couldn't imagine going through something like that. The poor man was entitled to a night of trying to forget.

After that everything had gone back to normal—whatever that was. She was still quarantined from the bar. Workmen were sanding walls and putting in new baseboards, getting ready for paint. That meant sawdust and fumes in the air. When the painters did their thing and it dried, she was going home. Oddly enough she wasn't all that anxious to leave. She was enjoying spending evenings with him—cooking, cleaning up the kitchen, watching TV (he was teaching her the basics of hockey) and just talking.

Clearly she'd been lonely, maybe even before her grandfather had died. Feeling lonely for someone her age to spend time with. Oh, who was she kidding? She had friends her own age—girlfriends. She hadn't spent time with a man in forever. That's all this feeling was. Friendship. With a man, a very good-looking one, who happened to be the father of her baby. The guy whom she hadn't liked very much and now found out she had been wrong about.

"This is stupid." Josh gave her a long-suffering and pitiful look.

She found out in their very first session that this was a recurring theme. "What's stupid?"

"Why do I need to know about Shakespeare? He's dead. For a long time now."

"I know. He was actually dead when I was in school. Back in prehistoric days," she said wryly. "When we wrote our papers with a hammer and chisel, on a rock."

He gave her an eye roll. "You're not that old."

"But by definition not that old means I am in fact old, though. Isn't that what you're saying?"

"Yeah." But he couldn't hide a grin.

"*Romeo and Juliet* is a classic. A tearjerker. The tragedy of star-crossed lovers."

"Because they were stupid," Josh said. "I don't get it. Why would a guy kill himself over a girl?"

"Why do you think?" Tess almost told him but this

should be a teachable moment. Even when he was rebelling against having to do work he hated.

"Because he didn't get the memo about her just being asleep and he thought she was dead. Stupid." He shrugged. "Romeo killed himself because he loved her?"

"Yes. And their families made it impossible for them to be together. And he didn't want to go on without her," Tess explained.

"What gets me is if he'd waited five minutes, she'd have been awake."

"So there's an argument for not making a hasty decision," she said. "Think things through and hang in there because it will almost surely get better."

"Are you talking about me now?" he asked suspiciously.

"Does it relate to your situation?" she asked.

"Maybe." He frowned for a moment.

"The truth is I didn't mean you. It was a note to myself."

"Why?"

Because it had been a rough year with her grandfather's illness and death. Financial problems with her business. Her unexpected pregnancy. Being off work. Worrying about money, especially with a baby on the way.

She met his impossibly young gaze. "Sometimes things are just hard and it feels like you can't catch a break."

He leaned back in the chair and stretched. "Yeah, tell me about it."

"The situation will get better. Sometimes doing nothing is best."

"That's what I did in English." He grinned.

Tess laughed. "And how's that working out for you?"

"Not great," he admitted.

"So sometimes doing nothing isn't an option."

"How do you know what to do?"

"Experience helps. Maturity. And—" she paused for theatrical effect then added "—reading and understanding Shakespeare."

He groaned dramatically. "It's so boring. I'd rather take Romeo's poison."

"Are you trying to tell me it's time for a break?" He had been working conscientiously since he'd arrived.

"Yes," he said simply.

"Okay. Are you hungry? Would you like a snack?"

"I could eat."

She stood and walked to the refrigerator. Because teenage boys had notoriously voracious appetites she'd stocked up on food. "How about a sandwich? Maybe fruit and some chips?"

"Yes. To all of it. I'm actually starving. And I have hockey practice in a little while."

Tess was dropping him at the rink because both of his parents were working. And they'd agreed not to take hockey away from Josh as long as he passed his classes. That was Leo's doing. He'd gotten involved with a kid on the edge, crying out for help. Because he'd been that kid. The thought of him paying it forward gave her a warm feeling, along with that weird sensation in her tummy every time an image of him popped into her mind.

She fixed Josh a ham sandwich on wheat bread, with mayonnaise, lettuce and tomato. After coring an apple and cutting it into slices, she put everything on a paper plate and brought it to him at the table, along with a bag of chips.

"Would you like water or soda with that?"

"Soda would be great."

She looked down at him, a lock of unruly hair falling over his forehead. She wanted to brush it back and wondered if that was her maternal instincts waking up. She hoped so. That would mean she had them, unlike her own mother, who had walked away and never looked back. From what he'd said, Leo would be a good dad. He didn't seem to have any doubts, but Tess had no frame of reference for this.

She grabbed a glass from the cupboard, put ice in it, then got a can of cola and poured it. After walking back to the table, she put it in front of Josh. He'd wolfed down the sandwich and was working on the apple.

"Leo is so awesome," he said.

"He seems like a good guy," she agreed.

"He's an awesome hockey player, too." He started spouting hockey statistics, records that still stood in that particular professional sport. "I'm going to be a hockey player just like him someday."

"That means playing in college." She remembered Leo talking about his trajectory to success.

"Yeah." Josh met her gaze warily. "You're going to tell me how I have to get my grades up so I can go to a school with a hockey team."

"It's like you can read my mind," she said.

"So, what's the deal between you and Leo?"

Apparently he'd decided on a quick change of subject, but the question caught her off guard. It shouldn't have. She was living in Leo's house with him, so she should expect curiosity. Along with the lack of a filter between the brain and mouth of a teenager. But the fact was she didn't have an articulate answer at the ready.

"I didn't catch that, what with your mouth full. Would you mind repeating?" she asked, stalling.

He chewed and swallowed. "I said—what's with you and Leo? Why are you living here? Are you guys a thing?"

"No," she said, dealing with the last question first.

But it wasn't that simple. They weren't dating, and never had. But there'd been sex—really wild, wonderful, quick and passionate sex. And she was carrying the baby to prove it. Her heart fluttered at the memory of being with him. More than once she'd thought about being with him again. In an actual bed.

"If you're not a thing, why are you staying here with him?" He took another apple slice and bit into it.

Just give him the facts. "I own a bar and Leo invested in it. He's now my partner." She sat across the table from him. "My apartment is above the bar and we're doing some remodeling. I had to move out temporarily and Leo offered me a room."

"Why?"

"So I didn't have to sleep on the street," she joked.

"No, I meant why did you have to move out?"

"Workmen were cutting wood. Sanding it. There's sawdust and other stuff floating around in the air. Plus there will be painting soon. So none of it is good if you're—"

"What?" he asked when she stopped.

She'd been about to say *pregnant.* Pretty soon she wouldn't be able to hide it, but that time wasn't now. The natural assumption would probably be that Leo was the father. But if she wasn't prepared to respond about her current living arrangement, she most definitely didn't want to talk about her condition.

Josh had some serious hero worship going on, and Leo was an exceptional role model. But this was a delicate subject. With luck she would be back in her place soon and there she could deal with it in her world, not Leo's.

But Josh had asked a question and needed an answer. "It's not good to be breathing that stuff in if you have pulmonary issues."

"That's like asthma and stuff, right?"

"And stuff," she agreed. "Allergies."

"Do you have that?" Josh bit into a chip and met her gaze as he chewed.

"No," she said honestly. "But Leo felt it was healthier for me to move out while the renovation is happening. And he has lots of room here."

"He's such an awesome dude."

"Yes, he is."

In more ways than she ever knew. She was teetering on the brink of a little hero worship of her own, and there was a problem with putting someone on a pedestal. The fall from said platform could be long and painful. And not just for the person on the pedestal. Whoever was feeling the awe could be in for a crash and burn, too.

Just because Leo wasn't a heartless bastard and was capable of genuine feelings didn't mean he could have feelings for her. He was pretty up front with the fact that he didn't plan on getting personal with her or having a relationship. For her own reasons she felt the same way.

A little while ago she'd told Josh that sometimes it was best to do nothing. She and Leo were a perfect example of that.

Leo was at the skating rink, in his office overlooking the ice. He was standing at the window, watching Josh's team gathering for practice. There were more parents than usual here with the kids—mostly moms, but dads, too. He knew something was going on that would affect this team and not in a good way. The adults were in groups, talking and looking very serious. The way a parent does when something negative is going to impact their child.

He saw Josh walk in, lugging his bulky hockey bag. Then he spotted Tess, just a step or two behind. He swore he felt his spirits lift and sort of levitate at the sight of her. Dropping the kid off was what she'd agreed to and he was getting a ride home with one of the other players. But Leo hadn't expected her to come inside.

Every protective instinct he had said not to go down there and talk to her. It was hard enough to pretend he didn't notice every sweet curve of her body when they were together under his roof. Nights were a spectacular challenge when he could picture her in a bed down the hall from his own. That should have been enough to keep him away.

Apparently it wasn't because the next thing he knew, he was heading downstairs, to where she was standing by the wall outside the ice.

"Hey," he said.

She smiled a particularly sunny smile. "Hey, yourself."

"How did tutoring go?"

"Oh, you know. Romeo and Juliet are dumb and English literature is boring."

He laughed. "I don't even know why I asked. If he was excited about it, his grades would be better."

"Yeah. But he's doing the work, which is the point. Someday he'll realize the importance of being a well-rounded human being but that's not today."

Leo watched the boys in their red-and-white jerseys burst through the opening in the half wall and onto the ice. School, family tension and all the bad stuff disappeared, and for the next hour it would be skating, teamwork and physical activity. "I was the same way at his age."

"He wants to be you when he grows up."

"God, I hope not. My life is a horrible warning."

"Not to him," she protested.

"If that's the path he chooses, he'll have to learn that hockey isn't everything." The pain of not seeing that certain little boy was with him every day. Wondering if he was happy. Did his biological dad love him enough? Did he even remember Leo?

Tess looked out on the ice, her gaze following Josh as he skated around. "I told him he better make Romeo and Juliet his new best friends if he wants to get into college like you did."

"Maybe that will help him see a point to the boring stuff now."

"Hopefully." She looked at the bleachers beyond the ice and at the facilities beyond the protective Plexiglas. "This is a nice place you have here. I planned to drop Josh off, not come inside. But I was curious."

"Would you like a tour?"

"Since I'm not working," she said wryly, "I've got nothing better to do."

"Try to keep the enthusiasm under control," he teased back. "It's not like I'm asking you to watch grass grow."

"Sorry. I didn't mean it like that."

"You should enjoy this time off. In about a week you'll be busier than ever and back home."

The thought of that didn't make him want to pump his arm in triumph. He must be more screwed up than he realized. Having her close put him on edge, and not having her around put him in a crap mood.

"I look forward to being busy again," she said. "So, are you going to give me the tour or not?"

"Follow me."

He showed her everything, starting with his office, which she called his window on the world. They looked at the skate-rental desk, then the equipment and apparel store. In the locker room she took one look at all the hockey bags and declared that a platoon of squirrels had crawled in there and the smell had killed them en masse.

In no uncertain terms she stated it wouldn't kill him to invest in a truckload of air freshener.

They ended up at the snack bar and he introduced her to Denise, who was working behind the counter.

"What can I get you?" the teen asked them.

"Coffee," he said. "Tess?"

"Hot chocolate." Her look was bittersweet when she added, "I don't think I've had it since I was a little girl and my grandfather made it for me."

"Anything to eat? Hot dog? Chili fries? Slice of pizza?" Denise asked him.

"No, thanks," he told her.

When she set the hot drinks on the counter, Tess started to pull out her wallet.

"It's on the house." Leo put his hand on hers, and a zap that felt a lot like static electricity zinged up his arm. It probably wasn't that but he didn't want to look too closely at why he'd felt it. Just another reminder that touching her was a no-no.

"Thanks." She took her cup and blew on the steam rising from it.

"Let's sit down over here. Unless you have plans." She'd told him that before the night of her grandfather's memorial, she hadn't been with a man in a very long time. That didn't stop him from feeling jealous about her with someone else in the future.

He didn't really believe Tess was lying, but it had happened to him once. Taking a chance on it not happening again was foolish.

"I have no plans." She picked a table and sat down on one of the chairs that faced the ice. "I like your place. But I'm wondering where the income stream is."

Leo took the seat across from her, his back to the practice going on. "Multiple sources. The snack bar, skate rental and sharpening. Even the equipment and clothing stores are all supported by selling time on the ice."

"How so?"

"There's admission for public skating. The hockey program is a big portion of revenue. Playing on ice is different from roller hockey. It's slippery."

"No kidding," she said with a laugh.

"Right. They have to learn to keep their balance."

"So the teams pay to practice."

"And play games." He glanced over his shoulder at the team now playing and frowned for a moment. "Every team is important to the bottom line. We do community clinics and giveaways at local parks to increase awareness of the sport and the team programs we offer. And it's not just business—it's a public service, in a way."

She nodded. "Because of kids like Josh."

"Yes."

She took a sip of her now-cooled hot chocolate. "It's also a safe environment with supervision, where kids can come and hang out."

"Yeah."

When his son was born—biology didn't matter; that boy would always be his son—Leo had been so excited about all of the things he would share with the little guy. He would take him on the ice and teach him to skate. Throw a football. Play catch with a baseball. So many hopes and dreams blew up in his face when he found out about the lie.

"I guess parental involvement is important," she said.

It was like she could read his mind. "Yes. Because of the expense, transportation and organization. Part of it is volunteer—coach, assistant coach, circulating information about practice and game times."

"That's quite a commitment."

A reflection of parents who loved their children. He knew the joy of that once, but now it was mostly pain. "Yeah. Without them the program doesn't work."

She nodded toward something going on behind him. "Don't look now but a whole bunch of those committed parents are headed in this direction. And some of the kids from Josh's team, too."

He turned and saw that she was right. Actually, he'd been expecting this. "Here we go…"

The group stopped in front of him and one of the dads stood a little ahead of the others. Leo guessed he was the spokesman.

"Hi, Mr. Wallace—"

"Call me Leo." He stood up and shook the man's hand.

"Okay." He cleared his throat. "Leo, I'm Bob Dempsey, assistant coach of the Predators. We've got a problem to discuss with you."

"Okay. What's up?"

"Our head coach. He had a job transfer, and long-distance coaching isn't going to work. As much as he regretted it, he had to quit. That leaves us in a bind." He blew out a breath. "I would take over, but the travel demands of my job mean half the time I can't be here for practices and games. If the boys don't have a coach, they have to forfeit."

"I know." Leo was looking at the boys and knew shock, anger and the unfairness of it all was cranking up all their youthful testosterone. He hated to see anyone not get to play. "What about one of the other dads? Or one of the moms?"

"No one else knows enough about the game or has the time, due to family and job obligations."

"That's a problem," Leo agreed.

"Josh Hutak came up with an idea and we thought it was worth a shot."

"Okay."

"Would you be willing to coach the boys? Obviously you know the game. You're one of the greats." Bob had a fanboy expression on his face. "You're here a lot. We were hoping you have the time and might consider doing it for them."

Leo had been afraid of this. It was true that he knew the game and had no family commitments. He glanced over his shoulder at Tess. At least not yet. Yeah, he'd reached out to Josh because running away from home made a big statement. But every one of these boys had a story. Every one of them could suck him in and they weren't his kids. He knew how it felt to get sucked in and lose out. His thing was to not get personally involved. The rink was just business. Being a coach was more.

"Look, Bob—"

The man held up his hand to stop the words. "Just think it over. Please. Don't say no yet."

He really wanted to say it, and the word was on the tip of his tongue. But Leo heard a chorus of voices and the words blended together into a pleading from the boys. The word *no* just didn't come out of his mouth.

He took the card with a phone number on it that the man held out. "Okay. I'll think it over."

"Thank you." Bob shook his hand again and led the group away.

He tucked the card into his shirt pocket for later. It would be easier to turn them down when he didn't have to look at their faces. Then he turned, and the look Tess was rocking told him where she fell on the issue.

"Don't you pile on," he warned her.

"I'm not sure what that means."

"It means that before our sports bar opens, I'm going to have to give you a crash course in the high points of sports." He put his hands on his hips. "I can't be their coach."

"You should."

"Why?" he demanded.

"You used to play hockey and know the game. You used to be coached, so there's that. You know how it's done." She tipped her head to the side and gave him what he thought of as her "kitten needing rescue" face. "You just told me that as far as revenue is concerned, you can't really afford to lose a team. And here's the big one. You told me that hockey was a lifeline when you were Josh's age. He's working his butt off to get his grades up so he can play. How do you tell him he can't because you're not willing to get involved?"

God, he hated how rational she was. She was using his words against him. But she'd never been more right.

He sighed. "Okay. I'll give Bob a call and tell him they've got a coach."

She smiled her approval at him. "You won't regret it."

He already did, because that smile touched him deep inside, in a place he'd sealed off to protect himself.

Chapter Ten

On the way home from the rink Tess stopped at the grocery store to pick up what she needed to make dinner. On the menu was oven-fried chicken, twice-baked potatoes and a salad with lots of fresh vegetables. When she got to Leo's house, he was on the phone in his home office so she jumped right into meal prep.

She wasn't working at her—correction *their*—business for another week, but at least she could make herself useful to earn her keep. After all, the man had given her a place to live.

She prepared the chicken on a cookie sheet after dipping it in egg, seasonings and cornflake crumbs. After putting it in the oven, she microwaved a couple of potatoes, scooped out the insides while saving the skin, and stirred butter, sour cream and chives into the mixture until it was just the right consistency. She sprinkled a little cheese on top and then slid them into the toaster oven to warm.

When the salad was made, she looked around the kitchen and realized she really felt at home here. And it had happened fast. The bar had been her home since she was six years old. Her apartment was cozy and you couldn't beat the commute to work. But it sure hadn't taken her long to settle in at Leo's house.

They said you didn't really know a person until you

lived with them, and she'd learned how true that was. She'd made it a point to get to know her baby's father. It was her obligation as a mother, right? Since she never really had one for most of her life, the fine print of the job was a little scary to her.

This kitchen was big, but felt even more ginormous without Leo in it. She wondered if he was still on the phone or just avoiding her. It was one thing to be lonely, all by herself in her apartment, but quite another when there was someone else here who sometimes treated her like an exotic-flu germ to be given a wide berth.

"I'll just go see about that," she said to herself. It was becoming a habit, talking to herself. And since he was here, she didn't have to. Not until she went back to her place.

She walked into his office, where he was actually still on the phone. While she waited, she settled into one of the chairs in front of his desk. There was a sheet of paper in front of him with a list of names and phone numbers. At the top it said "Predators Team Roster." Wow, Bob hadn't wasted any time getting out from under his coaching duties.

"The game is Saturday morning, at eight," he said into the phone. "I'd like Ethan to be at the rink thirty minutes early to loosen up, stretch and go over game strategy." He listened for a few moments and gave Tess a little wave. "Great. Oh, one more thing. Would you be able to bring water and energy drinks, maybe a snack?" He listened again and his mouth pulled tight. Classic Leo annoyance. "Okay. See you Saturday."

"I thought you were taking care of business in here," she said.

"I am. Hockey business."

"I guess you talked to Bob?"

"Yeah. He emailed the roster and game schedule."

"Since when is hours of phone time part of coaching?" She was feeling a little guilty for shaming him into this.

"What Bob failed to mention when he made his pitch is that the coach's wife was the team mom and did all the calls. So essentially we lost her, too."

"So you don't think she could be talked into staying behind to keep up the good work?"

He laughed. "Not likely, what with them being married and all."

"I had no idea this would be so time-consuming." More guilt crept in. "I'm sorry I said anything."

"That's right." His gaze narrowed on her, but his mouth curved up, a sign he was teasing. "You talked me into this. It's all your fault."

"Don't get crazy and say things you'll regret. Why don't you take a break. Dinner's almost ready."

"Something smells good," he said.

"It will be. You should have a beer. Chill out."

"That is a very good idea."

She stood and headed for the kitchen. "The least I can do is open one up for you."

"I'm right behind you."

Somehow she just *knew* he was staring at her butt as she walked away. Did he like what he saw? Did she want him to? Duh, no woman wanted a good-looking, former hockey-playing hunk of a man thinking her backside wasn't top quality. But did she want more? Could she ever risk that again? With something as important as a baby to worry about, she had an awesome excuse to put that question away, hopefully forever.

She opened the refrigerator and pulled out a longneck bottle of beer and then twisted off the cap. When Leo walked into the room, she handed it to him and he took a long drink of the cold liquid. In her line of work she'd seen a lot of men drink a lot of beers, but never was it as sexy as this. His neck muscles moved as he swallowed, and she barely held back a sigh of appreciation.

His big hand dwarfed the bottle he held. "This almost makes up for you getting me into this."

"I simply reminded you of what you already know."

"Sort of like my conscience talking." He took another drink of his beer. "And you're right about everything you said. I couldn't turn my back on Josh—or any of the other boys on the team, for that matter."

His words tugged at her heart. There was a time when she would have had a snarky comeback to everything he said, but now that she knew his painful past, her inner snark was rocking a whole lot of respect for this man.

It occurred to her—not for the first time—that he had way more experience with this parenting thing than she did. Since her résumé had zero kid know-how, of the two of them, he was practically an expert.

Once he knew for sure he was her baby's father, he was going to be a terrific dad. The question was, would she be a good mom?

"What's on your mind?" he asked.

She leaned back against the cupboards and folded her arms over her chest. As if that could stop him from seeing her deepest thoughts. "How do you know there's anything on my mind? I never said that."

"Your eyes are telling me."

She stared at him because she so badly wanted to cover her face with her hands. She was going soft on him and would prefer he not know how soft. The thing was, they were going to share a child, so there were fears she had that he would find out about anyway. She should probably confess.

"I think you're going to be a wonderful father," she started. "And you have no idea what a relief that is to me."

"Isn't that jumping the gun? First we need to have DNA done."

"Yeah, I get that. But it's going to be a match. That's not what worries me."

He set his beer on the island beside him, giving her and this subject his complete attention. "So, what is it you need to get off your chest?"

"I'm afraid I'm going to be a terrible mother." Her words came out in a rush.

"Are you mean to children? In the habit of tripping toddlers when they're learning to walk?"

"You tease, but this is a legitimate concern for me."

"Because your mother left you." It wasn't a question.

"Yes."

"But that's not all. And before you ask how I know that, your eyes are speaking volumes. Again." He shrugged. "I'm sensitive."

"Uh-huh. I wish my eyes would shut the heck up," she said wryly, then heaved a sigh. "But you're right. I'm a little nervous because everyone always said I look just like my mother. A clone. The spitting image."

"So she was beautiful, too." He leaned back against the counter as casual as you please. As if he told a girl every day that she was beautiful.

Well, that was unexpected. Nice, but still startling. And not her point. "She left me. A good mother doesn't abandon her child. The least she could do is stick around and take responsibility for screwing up her kid."

"You think you're messed up?"

"Don't you?"

"That's not the first thing about you that comes to

mind." His eyes went dark and intense for just a second. It was so quick, the change could be blamed on imagination.

Ignoring that was probably the best move, so she did. "What if I'm more like her than just looks? What if I can't handle the pressure of raising a child?"

"What if an asteroid crashes into the earth?"

"You joke, but I'm serious about this."

"I meant it in the context that you being a mom failure is about as likely as the asteroid/earth collision thing. Lighten up, Tess. You're going to do fine."

"How do you know?"

"Instinct."

"And yet there's still a doubt in your mind about whether the baby is yours." She held up a hand. "Scratch that. After what you went through, I can hardly blame you. But really—instinct?"

"If you weren't concerned, I would be worried. But you're all over this, which says there's nothing to worry about."

"I wish I had your confidence. And experience," she added.

"So get some."

"How? Rent a kid?"

"Funny," he said. "No, be the team mom."

"For your hockey team?"

"Yeah. You already know Josh. You've got time right now, until the bar's grand reopening."

Except for the fact that it could be a slippery personal slope working that closely with him on anything other than business, she didn't have a good reason to say no. "Other women get a plant or a dog to test their nurturing abilities but I get a hockey team?"

"Your mission, should you choose to accept it." He shrugged. "Deep end of the pool, Tess. Jump in."

"Okay. I'll do it." She blew out a long breath. "So, what are my eyes telling you now?"

He studied her closely. "Either dinner is ready or you want to choke me."

"How about both?"

"Good. I'm starving."

So was she. And hopefully he couldn't see how badly she wanted to kiss the living daylights out of him.

Leo had forgotten about the adrenaline rush of winning a hockey game. Since he broke his ankle, ending his pro career, he'd been trying to fill that void with women and sex. Watching the boys win was almost as good as playing on the winning team. Although as coach, technically he did, but he missed the rush of racing up and down the ice, working his ass off and the elation of scoring a goal.

Tess was standing beside him now, taking everything in with wide-eyed interest. She'd packed the ice chest with bottled water and energy drinks, and there was a bag with some empty-caloried treat that the kids would love. Parents and spectators were filing up the bleacher stairs, heading for the exit to wait for their kids outside, where it was warm. He watched the boys, now at center ice and skating slowly by members of the opposing team, shaking hands.

"Men are weird." With a puzzled look on her face, Tess stared at the team members passing each other.

"Should I be offended?"

"Oh…" She looked apologetic. "That didn't come out right."

"You think?"

"Sorry, it's just that I don't understand how one minute they're hitting each other, trying to take away that round black thing—"

"Puck," he said.

"Right. That. So they smack into someone—"

"It's called checking," he told her.

"Because that sounds so much better than *hit* or *smack*."

"It's a technical term. As in *checking* their forward progress down the ice."

"Anyway." She sighed. "They do that—checking—and knock each other on their butts. Now they're shaking hands and laughing. If that was me, I'd be so mad."

"Checking is part of the game. They all know it's not personal and when the game is over, it's over. Shaking hands teaches them sportsmanship. They learn to be gracious winners and good losers."

"Hmm. Lessons for being a grown-up," she mused.

"Exactly."

She nodded, then grinned. "I still think men are weird. Just saying."

"I could say the same about women, if I wasn't such a gentleman." He met her gaze and saw the teasing in hers. "You cry when you're happy or sad. Say 'fine' when you're anything but. And tell a guy you don't want to talk about it, then do a ten-minute monologue on why you're upset with a flower arrangement instead of a single rose."

"Because a single rose is more romantic," she said in a teasingly superior tone that also fell into the sassy range. "Everyone knows that."

"Guys don't."

"Because you're weird. I rest my case. Enough said."

She was a piece of work, and not in a bad way. After taking on team-mom duties, she'd jumped in with both feet. Phone calls got made, the kids showed up on time and she'd put together drinks and snacks for today's game. And that reminded him…

"Do not carry that ice chest back to the car."

"But it will be empty." Her face had the "men are weird" look on it again.

"I can't believe you were going to carry it full."

"It rolls," she defended.

"Not out of the car. Fortunately I was there." They'd come here together.

"I thought you had to get to the team and warm them up."

"There was time," he said.

"Well, I'm used to doing things on my own. And besides, I'm pregnant, not an invalid."

"Not a newsflash."

Before he could say more, the guys skated over and started taking bottled water and energy drinks out of the ice chest. It was too loud and raucous to have any conversation at all.

Tess watched the scene unfold, her eyes wide again. "They're like locusts, devouring every plant and blade of grass in their path. Leaving scorched earth behind."

"I think you're mixing your metaphors, but yeah. I can't argue with locusts." He took her by the shoulders and moved her several steps away. "Probably best to stand back, out of the way."

The kids thanked her politely, but as soon as they'd filed past, the roughhousing started up again. Good-natured arm punching, wrestling, grabbing someone around the neck. Guy fun. Male bonding.

Tess caught the corner of her bottom lip between her teeth. "Maybe I shouldn't have given them energy drinks. It looks like they have more than enough energy. Even after knocking each other down and chasing after that puck thing for an hour."

"Imagine if they hadn't released all that—let's call it youthful enthusiasm."

"Oh, dear God." She shuddered. "What you're telling me is that playing hockey is channeling their—let's call it vitality."

"Right. It has to go somewhere. This way they get exercise and learn how to get along with others, work together and handle disappointment when things don't go their way." God knew he'd needed that training when he had lost his family.

She was thoughtful for a moment, then said, "My grandfather took me to ballet classes."

"Last time I checked, that's not a team sport."

She laughed. "It checked all the same boxes as playing hockey."

"Still not a team endeavor."

"I beg to differ. There are other dancers in a production. Hello, *Swan Lake*. There's more than one swan." Her mouth curved up at the corners. "In case you're wondering, it wasn't Pat's idea. I begged him to let me do it and he finally gave in."

"Smart man."

"Yes, he was wise. But still weird like the rest of you," she said wryly.

"Are you ever going to let that go?"

"Maybe if this baby is a boy."

The baby. Even though her jeans were getting snug and she wore loose shirts, there were times he forgot she was pregnant. Like moments ago, when she teased and made him laugh. A few days before, she'd told him he would be a good father, and the words had made him feel good, before the pain of loss hit. He'd done his best with Chad because he loved that boy more than anything in the world. It wasn't enough and he was afraid to care that much again. To risk being shut out in the cold if it was taken away.

Tess shivered and she folded her arms over her chest. "I wish it was warmer in here."

"Hard to keep ice frozen that way." He grabbed his windbreaker off the bench and dragged it around her shoulders. "I should have warned you to wear a warmer jacket. Let's go get a hot chocolate at the snack bar."

"Twist my arm."

He called out to the boys hanging out on the bleachers nearby. "Good game, guys. See you at practice. Everyone clear on when it is?"

There was a chorus of "Yes, coach" and he nodded, then waved. Tess took the bag she'd brought the snacks in and used it to collect empty bottles and wrappers. Leo took the ice chest, and side by side they walked around the oval and over to the snack bar, where Denise was now working. He'd seen her just behind them in the bleachers, watching the game before she started her shift. He set the cooler by a table and then they walked up to the counter.

"Nice game, boss."

"The guys played well," he said, refusing to take any credit.

"Congrats on the first win of the season. This was the fifth game." She smiled. "So I think coaching might have made a difference."

He shrugged. "I just made a few adjustments in the lines. Spread around the stronger players. It was all them."

"If you say so. What can I get you?"

"A couple of hot chocolates."

"Make mine extra hot," Tess said.

"You got it." Denise walked away and came back with two coffee cups and protective sleeves. There was a generous amount of whipped cream on top of each. "Here you go."

Leo pulled out a bill to pay for them and she backed away.

"Seriously?" the teen said. "You're the boss. That should count for something."

"Let's just say I'm setting an example," he told her.

"I get it." She smiled as if suddenly understanding what the secret was. "You're trying to impress your girlfriend."

"What, I… No—"

"We're not a thing. Just friends." Tess jumped in to bail him out, but her smile was forced.

Leo knew that because she smiled a lot and he could tell real from fake. This was fake. And awkward.

"Oh. Sorry." Denise looked sheepish. "I thought I heard you say… Never mind. My mistake."

"That's okay." Tess took her cup, walked over to the table and sat down.

He waited for the sale to be rung up and get his change. He supposed anyone looking at them could come to the same erroneous conclusion that Denise had. After the game they'd been laughing and talking. He gave her his jacket, which was way too big for her. It reminded him how petite she was and how protective that made him feel.

The fact was, he was only her baby daddy. Maybe. That was yet to be determined. But was that all he was to her? Sometimes—a lot of times—it felt like more, and he was fighting the feeling with everything he had. But too often he got caught up in her and forgot to do that.

He sat down across from her. "Are you warmer now?"

"Yes. Thanks." She took a sip of her drink and there was a trace of whipped cream on her top lip.

This was one of those times when he did his level best to fight the urge to kiss that cream off her mouth. He blew out a long breath. "So, your first gig as team mom was a rousing success."

"Thanks." She smiled at the praise. "I brought drinks and snacks this week because soon I'll be back to work and won't be able to come to the games. Don't worry, though. I'll still make the phone calls, but I've assigned other moms and dads to snack duty, so it should be taken care of for you."

He nodded. "That means you'll be back in your place pretty soon."

Her bright look slipped for a second, then she regrouped and it was back with barely a flicker. "Yeah. I talked to Nate. One more day on the paint and two days to dry. He said one would be enough, but give it an extra day to be on the safe side."

Leo was all in favor of the safe side and getting back to it was what he wanted. He'd been thinking just a little while ago about trying to fill up the void inside him with women and sex. He'd had Tess only the one time, and then they had become business partners. Until today he hadn't given that void a single thought, and he had a bad feeling that was because of her.

"I bet you're anxious to have your own space back. Because, as you know, men are weird," he teased.

"I hope having me stay at your house wasn't an inconvenience for you."

It was, but not the way she meant. And soon there wouldn't be a problem. The sometime-feeling that they were more than friends would go away when she was no longer under his roof. But when he brought up the subject of her leaving, her smile disappeared. Real or fake, it was just gone.

And he didn't like that very much at all.

Chapter Eleven

Tess was at the bar, waiting for Carla. The workmen were gone for the day, which would disappoint her friend. She would miss seeing the brawny, tool-belt-wearing construction guys, but life was full of disappointments. Besides, her friend's job at Make Me a Match relied on algorithms and profiles filled out by clients, not face-to-face, man-on-the-street sightings.

The purpose of meeting here was to determine whether or not the paint smell was gone so Tess could come home. She'd asked Carla to come over and give her a second opinion. Nate thought it was fine but since he worked with it all the time, he had suggested she didn't take the chance that his sniff was sensitive enough for Tess's delicate condition.

There was a knock on the door before it opened and Carla poked her head in. "Hello."

"Hi." Tess walked over to give her a hug. "Thanks for coming by."

"No problem. There's no rush to get home. Mom is out with her friends from the Red Hat Society so she's not expecting me. I have a free evening."

"Translation—nothing better to do," Tess teased.

"Pretty much." She glanced around the now very open room. "Love what you've done with the place."

The cerulean walls looked pretty darn good if she did say so herself. "Really?"

"Yes." Carla studied her. "Don't you love it?"

"I think so. Hard to tell. I'm so emotionally connected that any change is like cutting my heart out. Leo assures me the modifications will make us competitive with the current trendy local hot spots."

"I can picture it." Carla looked around and nodded. "I like it for a meet for clients."

"Seriously? And we weren't on your list before?" Tess stared at her friend.

"Since I recently started working there after returning home in humiliation, it wasn't my decision." Carla looked sheepish. "I don't want to hurt your feelings, but before the renovation, this was a place the Red Hats would go, and those ladies are over fifty."

"And you don't have clients in that demographic?"

"Some," Carla admitted, "but our target clients are not retired or even close to it. They're high-powered professionals who want to find someone but are so wrapped up in their jobs, they're too busy to go through the time-consuming trial-and-error dating process to find that one special person."

"And you think *now* my business will measure up to your exacting standards?"

"Come on, Tess. Don't be that way. Change can be good. Shake things up."

"You sound like Leo," she grumbled. In her world things were shaken up quite enough, thank you very much.

"If everyone liked the same thing, all businesses would be just alike. Variety is key to finding your niche clientele. Different strokes for different folks. And all that."

"I thought you loved my grandfather's place."

"I do. And some of that is preserved." She looked at the bar that hadn't been touched in the renovation. "That doesn't mean it can't be made better. Keep what's working from the old and change what isn't to make it new."

"It's like you're channeling Leo right now," Tess said drily.

"Is that bad?"

"It's not good," Tess said.

Carla's eyes narrowed on her. "What's going on? Don't tell me nothing. Besides the fact that I know you practically as well as I know myself, you didn't ask me to meet you only to get my opinion on lingering paint fumes. Which, by the way, there aren't any. At least down here."

"Let's go up and check the apartment."

"You're stalling me, but okay."

Tess led the way upstairs, noting that there was no trace of a paint smell. She unlocked the door and stepped into her home. It felt as if she'd been gone years instead of weeks. And the space she'd always thought of as a warm and cozy haven smelled of loneliness. All she could think was that Leo's wide shoulders would barely fit in here.

"Can I get you anything?" she offered.

Carla shook her head. "It's sweet of you to offer, but you've been displaced and probably don't actually have anything."

"There is that…"

"So…" Carla settled herself on the floral-patterned love seat that separated the living area from her tiny kitchen.

It looked like Barbie's dream kitchen compared to Leo's ginormous one.

She sat in a club chair at a right angle to her friend. "Yeah, so…"

"What's got your pregnant panties in a twist?"

Leave it to her newly minted matchmaking friend to zero in on the heart of the problem. "Leo is coaching a teenage boys' hockey team. He stepped in when the existing coach had a job transfer. And I offered to help him because he also lost the team mom. She's married to the coach. Are you following?"

"Yeah. So far no problem. I guess there must be more." Carla had a knack for stating the obvious.

"I'm getting to it." She took a long breath. "After the game, Leo and I got hot chocolate at the rink's snack bar. The teenage girl behind the counter asked him if I was his girlfriend."

"And?"

"I told her I'm not."

Carla shrugged. "Still not seeing the problem."

"I'm still getting to it. So, here's the thing, I'm four months pregnant and still able to hide it with loose shirts. But I won't be able to do that much longer."

"Those of us who know and love you think you already aren't hiding it very well," her friend pointed out.

"Great. You get it, then," Tess said.

"No, not really."

"Okay. Let me spell it out for you. Very soon, when I'm out to here—" she held out her hand about a foot from her belly "—everyone will assume the baby is his."

"At the risk of stating the obvious," Carla said, her voice leaning toward sarcasm, "it is his."

"But we're not together," Tess cried. "What does that say about me?"

"You're human?" Carla gently suggested.

"Or I'm a slut."

"Stop it. Anyone who really knows you wouldn't believe that. And anyone else doesn't matter. They can go jump in the lake."

"I love you for that."

"I know." Her friend smiled. "Problem solved."

"No. It will soon be obvious that I'm going to have a baby. People will start asking questions. Like who's the lucky father? How do I answer that without lying? How do I say it was a big mistake and we're not together?"

"Do you want to be together?"

"What? Why would you ask that?" Tess said.

"Hmm. When someone answers a question with a question, something is definitely up."

"How do you know?"

"Questionnaires are a big part of my job. Individual answers to pair up people who we believe will make a personal connection. Sometimes the questions not answered reveal the most." There was a confident expression on her face. "I'm getting a vibe that you wouldn't mind being together. With him."

"As much as I hate to be the one to tell you this, your vibe can be wrong. You're not infallible."

"Agreed." Carla wasn't offended in the least. "But I'm right about this."

"No, you're not." Tess folded her arms over her chest.

"Hmm."

"Oh, brother. You're reading my body language, aren't you? You're going to say this is a classic protective pose and I'm closing myself off. Go ahead. Say it."

"I don't have to now." Her friend's grin was all-knowing. "Instead of putting you on the defensive, why don't you tell me about him. They say you never know someone until you live with them, so what's he like?"

"Different from what I first thought," Tess admitted. "He's not selfish, smug and arrogant."

She told her friend about him growing up in a home filled with conflict and unhappy parents. How his time on the ice was pretty much the only positive in his life. The way he'd taken Josh under his wing and prevented losing the hockey that he loved from becoming his punishment for a poor English grade. Tess felt the part about his wife cheating and taking away the child he loved like his own son was too personal to share. But what she told her friend was a pretty good sampling of reasons why she no longer believed he was a cocky, sweet-talking heartbreaker.

Carla nodded. "I wish you could have seen yourself just now when you were talking about him."

"If there's anything on my face, it's from lunch." Tess hoped saying so would make it true, because she didn't like where this conversation was going.

"Sorry, sweetie. You were trying to convince me of all his good qualities, wanting to persuade me he's a really good guy. There's absolutely no reason to do that unless you have feelings for him. Unless you like him."

"I do. But just as a friend." Tess tried to keep her voice neutral and not let on how desperately she hoped that statement was the truth.

"Okay."

"You don't believe me."

Carla's look was sympathetic. "I believe that you believe it's true."

"How can you know? The people you work with have filled out profiles because they're looking for love, not trying to avoid it."

"You would be surprised. Despite our best efforts, some matches don't work out. I keep a very large supply of tissues on hand for those occasions. There are times I feel like a counselor, helping someone get to the bottom of their relationship hang-ups."

"That's not what's going on with me."

That was exactly what was going on with her. She didn't believe Leo was like the boyfriend who cheated on her over and over. But Carla was confirming there were a lot of ways to be hurt.

Leo had said that she must be anxious to return to her own space. What she heard was that *he* was in a hurry to have his space all to himself again. It was time for her to move back and it was probably happening just in the nick of time. There was still a chance she could keep her heart in one piece.

Ever since Tess had moved into his house, Leo drove home with a sense of heightened anticipation. It was official. He couldn't avoid the fact that he looked forward to seeing her at the end of the day. It wasn't just about having someone there and not being alone. It was specifically *her*.

The renovations to the bar were finished except for a few minor details, and there wouldn't be any reason for her to stay with him. A couple days ago, after the boys' hockey game, he'd casually suggested that she must be anxious to be back in her space and maybe he'd been hoping she would say not really. That she was enjoying being with him. But she hadn't.

Leo liked being with her, talking about things. She had a quirky take on the world and made him laugh. Meals were eaten at the table, not in front of the TV, and there was conversation, too. They weren't having sex and that was killing him. He saw her every day and held her when she'd cried over changing the bar's name. At night, to know she was just down the hall and not be able to touch her was tearing him up. In spite of that, he still liked having her around. That got into tricky territory.

With all those thoughts running through his mind, the drive home from the ice rink seemed to flash by in seconds. Leo pulled into the driveway and noted that Tess was at the house. It was lit up like a church for Christmas services. A sigh of something that felt like contentment escaped him as he exited the car, and he tried not to hurry inside.

He told himself that he wasn't getting used to having her there, just enjoying the company while it lasted. And he really liked when he opened the front door and smelled something good cooking. His mouth started watering and he realized he was hungry, but not just for food.

Leo walked into the kitchen, where Tess was bent over in front of the oven, reaching inside to slide something out. He was treated to an amazing view of her butt. If only it was slightly less spectacular, he might want her less. Maybe.

He cleared his throat, partly not to startle her, but mostly because he wasn't sure he could speak in a normal voice. "Hi."

She straightened and glanced over her shoulder, then set a casserole on top of the stove. "There you are. I was wondering when you'd show up."

"Hockey practice went a little long."

She took off the oven mitts and faced him. "Those boys probably don't know how lucky they are that their coach owns the rink. I've heard that ice time is expensive. And they just got some at no extra charge."

"I wasn't late just because of practice. I stopped to talk to Josh while he was waiting for his dad to pick him up. Check on how he's doing."

"And?"

"School is better and his parents are…trying."

She frowned. "What does that mean?"

"I guess there's less tension in the house, at least in front of him. They've eased up on him about his grades. Oh, he said to tell you thanks for the help. He still doesn't like tutoring, but he passed the stupid *Romeo and Juliet* test."

"Shakespeare would be so flattered." She laughed.

He'd come to realize that the sound of her laughter magically relieved a long-day's worth of tension. The tightness in his neck and shoulders relaxed. He could only imagine what a "honey I'm home" kiss would do.

Enough with those thoughts.

"He's also embracing your philosophy."

"I have so many. Which philosophy would that be?"

"The one where you only have to remember this junk until the test and not for the rest of your life."

"Ah, that one. Heaven forbid." She nodded knowingly. "I left out the part where he probably can't delete it all from his brain as easily as he can from the computer."

"So he'll curse you when someday the words come out of his mouth, 'But soft, what light through yonder window breaks.'"

"'It is the east and Juliet is the sun,'" she finished. "So, you know from personal experience that no matter how hard you try, it will never leave you. I'm impressed."

"You remembered it, too."

"Only because I saw it recently from tutoring Josh." The expression on her face turned teasing. "In your case, maybe it's a pickup line."

Leo laughed because he'd never used that one and couldn't remember the last time he even needed a smooth opening with a woman. Then he stopped laughing when he realized he didn't even want to meet anyone new. Not since…

Tess interrupted that thought. "I was kidding. That wasn't a judgment on your social life. I don't think you're that guy."

"I know you don't." He had been, but wasn't now. "What's for dinner?"

"Shepherd's pie."

It was one of his favorites. "You remembered."

"I did."

"Hope it wasn't a lot of work."

"Not bad. And I made two. Froze one." She shrugged as if it was no big deal.

"Excellent." He looked around and the table was already set, a salad made. "Is there anything I can do to help?"

"Just have a seat and enjoy."

Leo enjoyed just looking at her, and it fed him somehow. If he was the kind of guy who was in touch with his feelings, he would say something about his soul. But he didn't even want to think that. Getting in that deep was a major violation that could land him in the penalty box for life.

Before he said something he would regret, he sat at the table and Tess brought over the casserole, then the salad. As usual she took the chair across from his. "So, what did you do today?"

"A lot of paperwork. Looked over reports for potential business investments."

"Really?" She put food on her plate and took a bite.

"Yeah. I have capital on hand and I'm hoping to find something that will give me a good return on the money."

"So the bar, ice rink and all your other financial projects aren't enough?"

"I like to keep busy. And this is my act two. I want to make it a success." He put food on his plate and tasted the shepherd's pie. The combination of beef, carrots, peas and mashed potatoes on top was heaven in his mouth. "This is really good."

"I'm glad you like it."

They ate in silence for a few moments. It was almost embarrassing the way he shoved food into his mouth but this sure beat anything he could have cooked. He was embracing the attitude of enjoying it while he could.

When the worst of his hunger was taken care of, he realized he hadn't asked what was going on with her. "How was your day?"

"Good." She finished chewing and swallowed. "I went by the bar."

"And?"

"It looks good." She met his gaze. "My friend Carla met me there and she likes it a lot. Better than before."

"Oh?"

"Yeah. She said the old atmosphere only appealed to members of the Red Hat Society."

"The who?"

"It's a group of women over fifty who get together for various activities. They all wear red hats." She frowned. "I never knew Carla felt that way about Granddad's place."

"Don't…" He stopped and looked at her.

"What?"

"I was going to say don't take it personally—then I remembered I was talking to you. It is personal."

She nodded. "But apparently you were right about it needing a makeover. And it looks good."

"So you wanted your friend's opinion on the results?"

"No. On the paint smell." Her much smaller portion was mostly gone but she speared a stray carrot with her fork. "To make sure it was okay for me to go back. I checked with Nate and he advised a second opinion because he smells it all the time. He's not sure his nose is as sensitive as someone who doesn't do that for a living."

"What's the verdict?" He kept his voice normal, natural, neutral. But it was an effort.

"Got the all clear." She set her fork on the plate. "I'm all packed and the guest room upstairs is all cleaned. After dinner, I'll tidy up the kitchen and then move back to my place."

If she'd smacked him in the gut with a two-by-four, he couldn't have been more surprised. But why? He'd known this was coming. He'd been aware it would be soon. And he should be happy, what with thinking about all that soul stuff just a while ago.

This time he forced a normal, natural, neutral expression on his face, then smiled. "You'll be happy to get back home, I'm sure."

"Yes." She sighed and looked around, maybe with a little longing in her eyes. "But this house is really nice. Although it wouldn't kill you to use some of that investment capital to invest in some furniture for the sad, empty rooms."

It was on the tip of his tongue to ask her to help him with that, but he held back. Because that would feel too much like decorating it for *her*. And this wasn't permanent. It was only ever meant to be temporary.

"I'll get around to finishing things around here one of these days."

"Admit it. You'll be glad to get rid of me and have your privacy back." She folded her arms on the table. "Then you can bring your dates back here for—whatever."

A few minutes ago she'd said she knew he wasn't that guy, and he knew the remark was meant to distance herself. It ticked him off when he should be grateful. A shrink would have a field day with him.

"I'll do that." He pushed his plate away with food left

on it. His appetite was gone. "And you don't have to clean up the kitchen. I can take care of it."

"I knew it," she said, pointing at him. "You *are* in a hurry to get rid of me." It was almost teasing, but that sentiment didn't quite reach her eyes.

He could do banter, too. It was a good place to hide and not let her see how he really felt. "Yeah. I didn't want to make you feel bad, but having you around has really been tough. And can we talk about your cooking?"

"If you hated that," she said, "you're going to hate the one in the freezer, too. At least it will remind you of how glad you are that I'm gone."

As if he needed reminding. Not that he was glad, but just that he should be. "What a relief that will be."

"Seriously, Leo. It was very gracious of you to give me a place to stay. I thank you, and your unborn child thanks you."

She stood and cleared her plate from the table. Leo did the same and together they did the dishes and put everything away as if she'd never been there.

"This is it." She looked up at him. "I'll go upstairs and get my suitcases."

"No. I'll get them. You shouldn't carry heavy stuff down the stairs."

"But I have to. My apartment above the bar is upstairs. It will be fine."

"I'll follow you over and bring them up for you." He held up a hand to stop her protest. "You can argue if you want, but it's a waste of breath. I won't take no for an answer."

"That's really sweet of you."

It wasn't sweet; it was crazy. He was a lunatic to prolong this. But maybe that was the point.

She actually had two suitcases and he carried them

both downstairs to her car. He followed her to the bar, where there was an outside entrance up to her place. After bringing everything inside for her, he stood just outside her door.

"So, I'll be seeing you," he said.

"Yes, you will. Good night, partner. And thanks again."

He nodded and turned away, jogging back down the stairs. No long goodbye. Simple, uncomplicated. And if that was the truth, why did he feel like crap for making it so easy for her to leave?

Chapter Twelve

Tess had agreed to tutor Josh and she intended to keep her word whether she was living under Leo's roof or not. And now she was not. But she wouldn't let a kid down just because she was missing his coach. A lot. It felt like more than a couple of days since he'd insisted on following her home and carrying her things upstairs. She felt out of sorts, as if she needed to do something. Like fix dinner and wait for him to come home.

Instead she was waiting for Josh. School got out a little while ago and he would be here soon to go over the paper he'd written about *The Great Gatsby.* This was certainly something his parents could handle, and Tess had talked to them to make sure they still wanted her involved. They did. He was sullen and abrasive when they tried to help so if she was willing, they couldn't thank her enough.

So Josh had emailed her the paper and she'd critiqued it after skimming the book she hadn't read since she was in the tenth grade. Leo was going to swing by and pick him up for hockey practice. It had all been arranged. At a given time he would be there, waiting in the parking lot so she wouldn't even see him. It was annoying how much that depressed her.

There was a knock on her door with the half window on top. Through the slit in the cotton curtains she could see it was Josh. He was on time. She opened the door to him and the hockey bag that was big enough for its own zip code.

She looked at it, then him. "Seriously?"

"I can't leave it outside. It might get ripped off and this equipment is expensive."

"But it's going to stink up my apartment," she said.

"Leo said he'd buy you a case of air freshener." The teenager had the audacity to grin.

"He already discussed this with you?"

Josh nodded. "Since you were back home, he told me to leave the bag outside. Then I reminded him that someone could take it in such a public place and he said that was a problem. Because the pads and skates and my helmet aren't cheap. My parents would kill me."

"And being dead would make it hard to play hockey," she said wryly.

"No kidding. That's when he said bringing it inside wasn't something that air freshener and open windows couldn't fix."

"He's very practical." She motioned him inside and pointed to a spot just beside the door for the bag. It was as far away from her as possible.

Josh did as instructed and then shut the door.

She said, "Would you like a snack?"

"If it's no trouble."

"I've got fruit and frozen taquitos. Some chips, too." She'd been grocery shopping and picked up extra that she knew he liked.

"Sounds awesome."

"Have a seat at the kitchen table. I've got your paper there. You did a good job. I just tweaked it. I used track changes and printed it out, then made some written comments in the margin. Mostly suggestions for different words, eliminating *stupid* and *dumb*, which are your favorites."

Instead of being offended, he grinned. "Well, those people in that book are dumb."

"I agree. They're also selfish, self-centered, deceitful characters who don't think about the consequences of their actions."

He looked pleased that she agreed with him. "And if they weren't so dumb, Gatsby wouldn't have gotten shot in his pool."

"It was a tragic end for a man who was simply desperate to fit in and be with the woman he loved."

"Like I said—dumb." He sat down at the table. "Just like *Romeo and Juliet*. Love made everybody stupid."

The kid was kind of insightful, she thought, setting some taquitos on a sheet of foil before sliding it into the toaster oven on the counter. "I guess that's pretty true."

"Why do writers write about people being morons?"

She gave that a ponder before answering. "I suppose it would be boring to read about a character who was perfect and never made a bad choice. Besides that, human beings are flawed."

"I guess."

She set a glass with ice and soda in front of him, then a plate with apple slices. Whether or not he'd enjoyed the book, at least he was thinking about it. And wasn't that the point? Maybe not the only one. "Great literature makes the reader feel something. Or should. Happy, sad, angry."

"I don't need to read for that to happen," he said. "My mom and dad do that all the time. Mostly the sad and mad part."

The timer went off and she took out the taquitos, put them on a plate and brought it over to the table before sitting across from him. "What makes you happy?"

"Hockey," he answered without hesitation. Then he started consuming apple slices while he looked thoughtful. "If it weren't for Leo, I wouldn't be able to play."

"He had a little help," she said wryly.

"Yeah. And I appreciate what you're doing. But he made it happen."

She couldn't argue with that. When Leo found this boy in the locker room at the ice rink, he could have called the police and social services. Somehow he knew that would have made things more messy and complicated. Instead she had suggested tutoring and he had talked her into being the tutor. Josh was on parental academic probation and was now bringing up his grade without giving up doing what he loved.

"He really did save your bacon," she agreed.

"And now he's my coach. And he's awesome. He just knows when to change up our lines for a game. When to bench a guy because his head's not in it. He takes the time to talk to me, explain stuff. And not just me. He does that with all the guys."

"That's really nice of him."

"It's not nice." He glanced at his paper with her handwritten comments. "Like you said there. That's a bland word."

So, he'd looked through it. She pressed her lips together to keep from laughing. "How would you describe him in one not-bland word?"

"Awesome." He didn't even have to think about it.

"That's a cliché," she said. "That's in your paper, too. Many, many times. There's this wonderful thing called a thesaurus that can supply various words that mean the same thing. Use your phone for more than playing games. I challenge you to give me something besides *awesome*."

He frowned thoughtfully as he ate. Finally he said, "I can't think of one. But he really cares. He *gets* me."

"Leo would like that. And I can't think of higher praise than—" Tess stopped because unexpected emotion clogged her throat.

"It's the truth. My parents don't understand anything."

"I'm going to stop you there, Josh. Your mom and dad love you or you wouldn't be here now to look over this paper with me. And if they hadn't agreed to this, you could kiss hockey goodbye."

"But all they do is lecture. Leo is cool about everything."

"He cares, but you are your parents' baby." She moved a hand protectively over her belly, where her own baby was growing. "He doesn't have the same emotional investment as they do. He came up with a solution that works for everyone. A compromise."

"He doesn't tell me what to do all the time."

"He actually does," she said. "It just doesn't feel that way."

"Maybe. He's just the best." Josh chewed and swallowed the last of his snack. Then he looked at her, and with all the angst of a fifteen-year-old in his eyes said, "I wish he was my dad."

And the hero-worship train kept on rolling, she thought. Maturity would give this teenager a different perspective on his parents and how much they cared. He didn't know yet how lucky he was to have both a mother and father who were there for him. If not for her grandfather, she didn't know what would have happened to her. And none of that minimized Leo's valuable contribution to Josh's future at a crossroads in his life.

Tess hadn't chosen to get pregnant and hadn't deliberately picked Leo for sex. It just sort of happened that night he'd put his arms around her, just being nice when she was crying. But even if she'd consciously put thought into the decision, she couldn't have selected a better man to be the father of her baby.

"Okay, fanboy," she teased, "let's dissect this paper and get you a really good grade on it."

For the next hour they went over each sentence, one at a time until every paragraph supported the one before it. They talked about more appropriate words and tightening the structure, eliminating content that was deadweight.

There was a knock on her door just as they reached the end of the paper. She glanced at the digital clock on the microwave. "Time flies when you're having fun."

"It's Leo," Josh said, looking through the window. "Oh, man, I'm late."

It was definitely Leo, and her heart responded the way it always did when she saw him. There was a painful squeeze and her belly tightened. Before she could make a move, Josh jumped up to open the door.

"We were working and I didn't notice the time. I should have been waiting in the parking lot. I'm sorry."

"No big deal, kid." Leo looked at her, then back at Josh. "Tutoring must be going well if you forgot to watch the clock."

The teen shrugged nonchalantly. "It's okay."

"I refuse to take that personally," she teased. "If I say so myself, it was awesome."

"Cliché." Josh pointed at her.

"I rest my case," she told Leo. "Now he's the language police. I think his paper will earn a good grade and raise his overall score in the class. In my humble opinion his hockey career is saved. My work here is done."

"Good." Leo glanced at the ginormous bag by the door.

"Hey, kid, why don't you grab that and meet me at the car."

"Okay." He started to, then turned back to Tess and gave her a spontaneous hug. "Thanks for everything. And the snacks were really good, too."

"You're welcome."

He scooped up the handles and hefted the bag over his shoulder, then waved and walked out the door.

Tess was going to miss him. She sighed, then met Leo's gaze. "I'm sorry you had to come up."

"I needed to talk to you anyway."

"First, where's my case of air freshener?"

He grinned. "It's on order."

"That does me no good. I'll just have to open windows." She leaned against the open door. "Okay, your turn. What did you want to talk about?"

"I can't right now. There are a bunch of fourteen- and fifteen-year-olds waiting for me at the rink and they need supervision."

"Right, so—"

"I wanted to set up a time to meet. We're having a grand reopening soon and we need to nail down some things. Are you free in the morning?"

"Yeah. I'll be here waiting for the new furniture to be delivered."

"How about ten?"

"Works for me," she said.

"Good. I'll see you then." He glanced outside. "I have to go."

"Right. Have a good practice. See you tomorrow."

The thrill of anticipation coursed through her until she checked the feeling. It felt a little like that scene from the movie *Oliver!* with the titular hungry orphan holding up his empty bowl and asking for more, please. How pathetic was she?

A short time ago she'd thought about what a great father he would be. And he would. But that was all about the baby. It had nothing to do with her. And wasn't it unfortunate that the two of them had more personal baggage than would fit in Josh's hockey bag? Neither of them wanted a relationship. And that was a darn shame because she'd always wanted a traditional family.

While living with him, she'd begun to think there was chemistry between them. That hope imploded when she saw how happy he was for her to go back home.

It was for the best. Josh's study of literature led him to the conclusion that people did stupid things because of love. No way was she going to be dumb again. So, she and Leo and the baby wouldn't be the traditional family she'd always dreamed of, but there would be a mother and father in the picture. That was more than she'd had. It would just have to be enough.

Leo couldn't put it off any longer. The grand reopening of the bar was happening soon and they needed to decide on a name. That's the main thing he'd wanted to talk with Tess about today, and he was on his way over there now. As much as he was looking forward to seeing her, no way he wanted her upset. And he knew this discussion would do that. When he had raised the subject, she had cried and he hadn't been able to ignore the compulsion to protect and comfort her. The first time it had happened was the reason he was in baby-daddy limbo now.

He drove into the parking lot and saw a big delivery truck backed up to the door. Tess was talking to two big, burly guys and pointing at something inside. She was wearing black yoga pants and a tank top. The outfit highlighted that her belly was growing rounder every day. The baby was getting bigger and would be here soon. And Tess looked both cute and sexy as hell.

It was a damn good thing he wasn't going to be alone with her because if she shed tears, he was going to comfort her. If he put his arms around her, he didn't think he would be able to resist kissing her. But there was no point in borrowing trouble. Maybe she would be okay with this change.

He got out of the car and walked over to her. "Morning."

"Hi, Leo." She looked up at him and used her hand to shade her eyes from the sun. "The new furniture is here."

"I noticed, what with the big delivery truck and all," he said wryly.

Side by side they watched barstools, love seats, club chairs, end tables and dining sets being taken off the truck.

"How was practice?" she asked.

"Good. I see improvement."

"That's great. Josh was singing your coaching praises yesterday. He talked about changing up lines and knowing when someone's head wasn't in the game."

He met her gaze. "There are a lot of factors that go into pulling a team together. This one has a lot of potential. No offense to the last coach, but it helps to have played the game."

"Probably, but you also have to be a leader, one the kids respect, or there's no way you're going to pull them together." She smiled. "According to Josh, you have wings, a halo and you walk on water."

"Fortunately it's frozen or I'd sink like a stone."

She laughed. "FYI, some of Nate's guys are here tying up loose ends. They're putting up all the flat-screen TVs."

"Yeah, he called me."

After a few moments of silence she said, "Enough small talk. What's so important that you had to make an appointment to talk about it?"

"Hmm?"

"Yesterday, when you picked up Josh, you said we needed to discuss something."

He actually remembered and was merely stalling. "Right. It's just last-minute details. It can wait until this is done." He angled his head toward the growing array of eclectic furniture accumulating on the sidewalk.

Nervously, she caught her top lip between her teeth. "I hope everything looks okay when they get it inside. Now that I see it, I'm not sure the furnishings all go together. Maybe blending new with what was already here was not the best way to go. I don't want to let my grandfather down."

"You won't," he reassured her.

"How can you be sure?"

"Because I won't let that happen. He knew that when he asked me to invest. This is going to be the 'in spot.' The happening place for all occasions."

"Date night and bachelor parties? Seems like sort of a conflict of interest to me."

"We've opened the window wider to appeal to a more diverse clientele. Birthday parties, family reunions, bachelorette parties, too."

"Baby showers?" She looked ruefully at her tummy.

"Why not?"

"I'm not sure we can handle the food for those types of events. I know I gave you a hard time about a chef, but you might be onto something."

"We can cater at first, if necessary," he said. "One of our first new hires should be a chef. Someone creative with food, who can turn pub cuisine into something special."

"What do you mean 'first hires'?" she asked. "You kept everyone on the payroll during renovations. And I promised Brandon he had a job when we reopened. He needs it until he gets his business degree from UCLA."

"I'm counting on him," Leo assured her. "But he *is* going to graduate next year and will probably leave. We need to train someone now to take over. And then there's replacing you."

"Hey, I'm a partner." She stared at him. "Not going anywhere."

"But you're having a baby." He indicated the bump of her tummy that proved his point. "You won't be able to fill in. At least not at a moment's notice anyway."

Leo remembered the turmoil of having a new baby in the house. Sleepless nights. Colic and crying. Teething and crying. The needs were varied, immediate and required attention. When he had to be out of town for games or other professional commitments, guilt and worry became his new best friends. His ex-wife wasn't a bad mother, but her parenting philosophy allowed for more crying and less cuddling. His way of thinking was just the opposite.

It was on the tip of his tongue to ask Tess's opinion until he reminded himself he didn't have to. Not yet. Not until the baby was born and he had proof that he was the biological father. The only privileges he had now were what she allowed. He wasn't going to get sucked in and care until a test said he had as much right to the child as she did.

All the furniture was finally out of the truck, and one of the delivery guys asked her a question about where to put it.

"Let's start with the barstools. The new ones will be intermingled. Take away half of the existing ones and place them old, new, old, new."

"You got it," number one big guy said. "You want us to take away the old ones?"

There was regret in her eyes when she nodded. "But save two. I'm going to put them upstairs in my apartment. Keepsakes."

"Will do," he said. "I'll have Vince carry them up for you."

"That's all right. I can do it."

"Lady, in your condition you shouldn't be carrying stuff like that at all. Especially up the stairs."

"He's right." Leo made a mental note to give these guys a nice tip.

Tess turned on him. "Did you say something to them about the baby?"

"I just got here. And, no, I didn't make a phone call. It's obvious."

"On the up side, at least they didn't assume I was just putting on weight," she said.

Not a chance, he thought. She was still curvy in all the right places, all the best ones. He would give almost anything to explore them. Just the fact that idea crossed his mind made him double down on his promise to not go to hell where Tess was concerned.

He instructed them to work around the two men hanging the flat-screen TV. Then they followed big guy number one and Vince inside, and Tess showed them how she wanted the lounge furniture arranged. She pointed out the dining area, where the tables and chairs would go, and studied the center bar with a critical eye, particularly the blending of chairs. "I wasn't sure these would work together, but it's okay."

Kind of like the two of them, he thought. "It looks better than okay."

They observed as the lounge took shape and there was a smile on her face. It didn't take long to arrange the tables and chairs in the separate dining area. She walked around the place, nodding her approval.

"It's not awful," she told him.

"High praise coming from you. I guess that's a hat trick for me." He saw her blank expression. "Hockey term. Three goals by one player in a single game."

"Okay, then. You get one of those."

While Vince took her keepsake barstools up to her apartment, big guy number one came over with a work order that needed a signature. Leo did that and gave him a check and a generous tip. "Great job."

"Thanks."

They shook hands and the men left the building just as Nate's construction guys came out of the lounge and left.

Tess was still strolling around, taking stock of the interior, as if she'd moved into a new house. "The walls are so bare. It looks so different."

"Good different or bad?"

"Not sure yet. But I guess it is what it is."

"Yeah, about that—"

"Now you can talk to me about whatever it is you didn't want to bring up in front of strangers." She met his gaze and there was nothing in her expression that hinted at what she was thinking. "It's about the name change, right?"

"Yeah. We need to make a decision. It should be on the window when we reopen."

"I know." There was a trace of sadness in her voice.

"What are your thoughts?"

"Keep the old one." Her tone was part teasing, part hopeful. "Just kidding. Mostly."

"I know this is difficult." The last time he brought it up she cried and he hated that.

"At least you warned me. And your reasoning is sound." She sighed. "So, I've been thinking… Here's my list, in no particular order and not especially good. The Corner Pub. Pub on the Corner. Cheers. No One Knows Your Name. No Name. Tess's Tavern. Tess and Leo's Tavern."

"Hmm." At least she hadn't left him out, much as she probably wanted to. "I know we're mixing old and new but I think those are a little too much on the new side."

"Do you have a better idea?"

"I think so." He hoped she approved, because he had work orders pending with a tentative new name. "What do you think about Patrick's Place?"

She didn't say anything, just let the words hang there in the air, where her grandfather had built his business from the ground up. Her eyes glistened with unshed tears and he was about to take it back.

"You don't like it. No problem. We can brainstorm some more. I have a list, too—"

"No." She put the tips of her fingers over her mouth for a moment. "It's absolutely perfect. Granddad would love it."

"Okay, then," he said.

That was a relief, until it wasn't. His arms ached to hold her. He'd almost counted on it but didn't have to after all. What kind of a scumbag was he for wishing she had cried? Now there was no excuse to hold her. Even worse, he wanted to kiss her. Not only was he a scumbag; he was a stupid one. He was on the verge of breaking his rule about getting personally involved.

The definition of *insanity* was doing the same thing and expecting a different result. Thank goodness the busywork to get Patrick's Place open was almost done. As soon as the doors were open again, he could back off and let her run the show.

He wouldn't have to see her, and eventually she would be out of his system.

Chapter Thirteen

"What if no one shows up?" Tess said to Leo. They were standing by the bar, staring at the front door that hadn't budged, even though they'd only officially reopened thirty seconds ago.

Patrick's Place was more than ready and she was primed for action, but panic was setting in. "What if this is an epic fail and we go bankrupt? I'll be an unemployed single mom. What am I going to do then?"

"Take a breath." He put his hands on her upper arms and gave her a reassuring squeeze before letting her go. "One step at a time. We've made all the right moves. Advertising in the local paper and TV spots. Coupons. Invitations to friends and former customers. They'll come. We'll have at least one spectacular night."

"You're being way too rational," she said before his words sank in. "One? Oh, God. What if no one comes back ever? Without repeat business, we'll fall on our faces—"

"This is just wrong," he said. "The world has gone mad. Everything is turned upside down."

She blinked at him. "What are you talking about?"

"I'm usually the 'glass half empty' guy and you're Priscilla Perky. What's up with this reversal of roles?"

Tess realized he was right. "I'm sorry. I just don't want to let Granddad down."

Hanging on the wall behind the bar was a grouping of

framed photos. One of a young Patrick Morrow with a shovel in an empty lot. Another picture was Pat and her grandmother, Mary, staring lovingly into each other's eyes, right here where Tess was standing with Leo. Still another showed her grandfather with his arm around her shoulders when she'd turned twenty-one and could actually work with customers.

"I don't want to disappoint him." Her voice was thick with emotion.

"That could never happen." Leo moved closer and gently nudged her chin up so she'd look at him. "He loved you more than anything in the world. You never disappointed him, then or now."

"I miss him."

"Me, too. But I believe he's here, Tess. Watching over the place. And you."

She nodded. "Thanks for the pep talk. I bet you're a really good coach."

"I am. Humble, too." His charming grin unleashed nerves of a different kind.

"It's showtime." Brandon walked behind the bar and dumped a bucket of ice into the sink back there. "The caterer and servers are ready to do their thing."

She and Leo had decided to hire someone for this event so Tess could schmooze. Bridgette Mansfield had been hired as the chef and would be helping out tonight, then take over during regular business hours. For now there were a couple of new menu items, and she was developing more.

The front door opened and in walked Carla and Jamie. They both gave her a hug, then stared at Leo.

"Are you going to introduce us?" Carla asked with her customary directness.

Tess couldn't believe her friends hadn't been introduced to him. But the memorial was the only time their paths had crossed, and she hadn't been at her best that day.

Carla spoke up first. "You were at Pat's memorial, but we didn't speak. I'm Carla Kellerman."

"Jamie Webber." Her other friend shook his hand.

"Nice to meet you both." Leo grinned. "I was just telling Tess that her friends wouldn't let her down."

"Speaking of letdowns," Jamie said, "I invited Bill to come tonight, but he was called back to the Seattle office."

Before Tess could respond with sympathy, the door opened again and a group of people walked in. They looked around and then headed to the bar, where Brandon was waiting for them. She recognized a few who were regulars when her grandfather was still alive.

"I'm going to mingle." Tess hugged both of her friends. "Bless you both for coming tonight. Leo will give you the tour."

"Happy to."

He gave them his most charming smile and had never looked more handsome. In jeans, a powder blue dress shirt and navy sports jacket, he was every hunky inch the successful financial professional. She remembered her friends saying that a sports bar would be a good place to meet guys. A flash of irritation jolted her and she recognized it as a bit of jealousy. Not for Carla and Jamie. But other women.

It was inevitable that there would be, because his marrying mind-set had been annihilated by the bitch who had lied about being pregnant with his child. His parents hadn't helped either. And it was incredibly sad because he was a decent, wonderful man with a giant capacity for caring. He deserved better; he deserved to be happy.

"Tess Morrow—"

She tore her gaze from Leo's back and looked toward

the bar. She smiled at the familiar face of an older man who had his choice of seats and had picked one of the old barstools. She walked over and hugged him. "John Alexander."

"Hi, honey. Good to see you again."

The man was a silver-haired widower in his sixties. Her grandfather had befriended him after his wife had died. He was lonely and came in frequently for a beer and conversation. Group therapy for the two of them, Pat had always joked.

"It's good to see you," she said. "Thanks for coming."

"Wouldn't miss it for the world."

"I have to admit to a little anxiety about this grand re-opening. I was afraid it would go down in flames." She looked around the room that already held a respectable number of people. The place was big but from where she stood, she could see what was going on. Patrick's Place was filling up nicely.

The door was opening every few minutes to admit more customers. The temporary help was circulating with appetizers, taking orders and serving drinks. Some people were at tables in the dining area while others made themselves comfortable in the lounge to watch the hockey game on TV. Stanley Cup playoffs, Leo had told her.

"I don't think there's anything to worry about," John said. "For what it's worth, I think Pat would have really liked what you've done with the place."

This man had known her grandfather pretty well and his opinion mattered very much to her. "Really?"

He nodded. "Without a doubt."

"It makes me happy you'd say so."

"It's like home away from home. Companions. A meal. Watch some sports with other fans, let off a little steam." He nodded again. "The Pub always had it but now there's a more with-it, welcoming vibe, if you know what I mean."

"Thanks to Leo." This was his idea. She glanced around and spotted him chatting up the hockey fans watching the game and requesting his autograph, which he scribbled on the cocktail napkins prominently displaying the name Patrick's Place.

"It doesn't hurt that your partner is Leo 'The Wall' Wallace."

"I see you've heard of him."

"Anyone who follows the sport has." John took a sip of the beer Brandon had put in front of him. "It would seem congratulations are in order on another front, too."

She dragged her gaze away from her gaze-worthy partner. "Hmm?"

"The baby."

Holy crap!

With everything else on her mind, she'd forgotten. And when she'd thought about the baby earlier, she'd assumed her loose white blouse over jeans would conceal her condition. Apparently not. And there was no point in blowing off the comment. He was a loyal customer who would be back, and the baby was going to grow until there was no way to hide it.

"Thank you," she said. "It was a surprise."

"Is Leo excited about becoming a father?" There was a twinkle in the older man's eyes.

Double holy crap! He couldn't possibly know. The question was—why in the world would he jump to that conclusion? She looked around and then lowered her voice so no one nearby could hear. "Why in the world would you think it's Leo's baby?"

"A feeling." He smiled. "Because of the way you keep looking at him."

"Oh?" Play it cool, she told herself. "How am I looking at him?"

"The way I did at my Janie. And Pat looked at your grandmother like that, too." He shrugged. "So maybe it's more of an educated guess."

"Anyone who knows me would be surprised by this, but I really don't know what to say." No way would Leo want this talked about. Maybe after a DNA test confirmed the truth, but definitely not here or now.

"Pat would be proud to be a great grandfather. He was fond of Leo, like a son—or grandson."

That made her so happy, and weepy, but she had to keep that part inside. "John, I don't—"

"Don't worry, honey. Your secret is safe with me." He lifted his beer glass. "Let's drink to the success of your new endeavor."

"To my endeavors," she echoed. Which included the business and the bun in the oven.

Tess kissed his cheek, then moved on. She greeted familiar faces and planted the seeds of friendship with strangers. Leo had been right. The place was crowded and everyone seemed to be having a good time. Until closing, Tess and Leo circulated, shaking hands, serving appetizers and drinks, making conversation and welcoming customers they hoped would become regulars.

After the employees cleaned up, they urged them to go home and get some rest, then locked the place up. She was alone with Leo, standing by the front door. Again.

He looked down at her. "I feel as if I just played a hockey game with double overtime."

Tess understood the sentiment even though she had no frame of reference for it. "Being nice to people is exhausting, but I'd say it went well."

"You were amazing."

"Thanks. You weren't so bad yourself." She looked down at his big hands. "Did you get carpal tunnel from signing autographs?"

He flexed his fingers. "Nope. All good."

"I heard from a lot of people—new customers—that they came in just to see the legendary Leo Wallace."

"Really?" He pretended surprise and it was the cutest thing ever.

"Own the honor, Wallace. You can't really pull off humble, so… Just saying."

He grinned. "I feel so used. Nothing but a marketing tool."

She laughed, but a yawn took over in spite of her efforts to suppress it. "Sorry. It's not the company. Just a long, busy day."

"And you're pregnant."

"Not breaking news." Not to her, but John had guessed.

"How are you holding up?"

"Not too bad. Although my feet hurt and I'm afraid to sit down because I may never get up."

"You need to go upstairs," he said. "Get some rest."

"I will. As soon as my feet stop throbbing. Go on home. I'll turn out the lights."

"As soon as I know you're settled upstairs." He moved closer, then scooped her into his arms.

Now it wasn't just her feet throbbing. Her pulse was going a mile a minute and she could hardly breathe. This was super dangerous—to her heart and his back.

"Put me down, Leo." Right words but there was no oomph behind them. She slid her arms around his neck.

"I will. As soon as you're in your apartment, safe and sound."

He carried her up the stairs as if she barely weighed anything, though the scale at the doctor's office told her once a month that that wasn't true. Stopping at her door, he removed his arm from beneath her legs and let them slide to the floor.

"Do you have the key?"

Right! He couldn't open it with his arms full of her.

"In my pocket." She fished it out and opened the door. "That was very chivalrous of you. Foolhardy but so gallant. Thanks."

"You're welcome."

The deep voice and completely adorable smile made her stomach flutter. Then she realized it wasn't *that*. The baby was moving. "Oh, wow—"

"What? Is something wrong?"

"No. Just the opposite. The baby moved. He's doing that a lot now. Feel." She took his big hand and put it on her abdomen. As if on cue, the baby moved again and it felt like big bubbles rippling inside her. "Did you feel that?"

"Yes."

His voice was ragged and at first she thought he was irritated that she would assume he wanted to feel the baby kick, or be involved at all. But that was before she saw the intensity on his face, read the hunger in his eyes and *knew*. Her heart started hammering.

And then he kissed her.

Leo ached to have her. When she took his hand and he felt the baby move, probably his baby, it was more than he could stand. His choices were to kiss her or implode. So he kissed her.

Those full lips were even softer than he remembered. He tunneled his fingers into her hair and cupped her cheek in his palm. When he traced her lips with the tip of his tongue, she opened to him and he explored the sweet moistness as his breathing escalated.

Tess put her arms around his neck and pressed herself closer to him. What with the pregnancy, her belly was more rounded now and her breasts fuller. Sexy curves made even sexier by the life growing inside her. More than his next breath, he wanted to hold her naked body against his own.

"Tess?" He took her arms from his shoulders, but couldn't end the contact and held her hands. "Should I not have done that?"

"What? Kiss me?"

He nodded. "Did I overstep? Read this—whatever it is between us—wrong? If you don't want this, I'll back off and we never have to mention it again."

"Are you saying you don't want me?"

"God, no." He squeezed her hands just a little tighter, as though she'd pulled away and he couldn't let her go. "I just wanted to… It's just that we agreed… You know, that this would be all business, no pleasure."

Her dark eyes sparkled with humor and passion, and she had never looked more beautiful. "Then we will take no pleasure from it."

Oh, thank God. He grinned. "Agreed."

Leo touched his mouth to hers again, trailing kisses over her cheek and neck, then nibbling her earlobe. She gasped and shivered, and tilted her head to the side, giving him license to take what he wanted. And he did. Until he couldn't stand it anymore.

"Where's your bedroom?" he asked.

She stared at him with glazed eyes. "What?"

"Room? Bed? Don't get me wrong. The table wasn't bad. But this should be done in a proper bed."

"Hmm. I never thought of my bed as proper." She

grinned and took his hand. "Let's go find out if you're right about it."

Tess led him through a doorway and into the next room. The bed was big, fluffy and feminine, with a flower print on the spread. Throw pillows of all sizes and shapes, in shades of pink, green and maroon, were neatly displayed. And not so neatly tossed aside when she started to pull down the covers, spread and all. Light trickled in from the other room, enough for him to see her slide her top over her head and drop it on the floor. From the waist up all she had on was a lacy white bra.

Leo was afraid he'd swallowed his tongue. She was so beautiful. He reached out and cupped her breasts in both hands. Through the lace, he brushed his thumbs over the tips and she gasped once, then moaned with pleasure. She was sensitive and responsive to his touch. And he was sensitive and responsive to the sensual sounds she was making.

His hands shook when he reached behind her and released the hooks on that sexy little scrap of material. The wisp slid to her feet and he stared at the beauty of her.

Her breathing was unsteady when she said, "You look like you're taking pleasure from this."

"No. I swear. Not enjoying this at all." He could barely get the words out and heard the ragged edges of his own voice.

"Okay. Just checking," she whispered. "And I'm not going to like this at all either."

She reached out and undid the buttons on his shirt, one by one, with excruciating slowness. It took every ounce of his willpower not to push her hands aside and rip the thing over his head. Finally the front was open and she rested her palms on his bare chest, touching him the way he'd touched her. It had been months since he'd had sex with her and he was afraid if he didn't hurry things along, this would go very badly.

"I'm hating this so much, but can we get to the part that is the least pleasurable?"

He wasn't proud of the desperation in his voice but it couldn't be helped. He kicked off his shoes, took off his socks and unbuckled his belt before sliding off his jeans and boxers.

Her eyes widened in approval as she gave him a once-over, then fanned herself by waving a hand in front of her face. "At the risk of totally blowing our agreement, you are not hard on the eyes."

"I aim to be adequate."

She smiled, then slid off her pants and stood in front of him without a stitch on. Leo could hardly breathe. Her legs were long, smooth and shapely. The rounded belly and full breasts were the essence of femininity and the most beautiful sight he'd ever seen.

"Say something."

"Not sure…" He cleared his throat. "I know we agreed no pleasure but you are—"

"Don't say it."

"Wait. First you tell me to talk—now I can't?" He shook his head. "I have to tell you. You are exquisite."

Her eyes filled with tears. "Thank you."

He tugged her into his arms and couldn't believe how soft her skin felt, how sweet her curves were against his chest. He kissed her long and deeply as he swept his hand over the curve of her waist and thighs. Slowly he moved his palm over her abdomen, lower to that place between her legs and slid one finger inside her.

She cried out with desire and her knees buckled. "Oh, Leo, I need you. Now."

Didn't have to ask him twice. He swung her into his

arms and settled her in the center of her big, soft bed. He got in beside her and pulled her close, touching her everywhere, kissing her until they both couldn't bear it another second.

He rolled over her, taking his weight on his forearms, and she opened her legs without hesitation, welcoming him to her. He entered her slowly, willing himself to take his time, but Tess was impatient. She arched her hips and wrapped her legs around his waist, urging him to go faster. He thrust once, twice and then she cried out and clung to him, her body trembling with pleasure.

The thought made him smile as he held her until the shudders subsided. Then he thrust slowly into her again, but there was no holding back now and his own release rocked him to his core. He buried his face in her neck and they held on to each other for a long time.

When he could think clearly, he rolled off her. "I must be crushing you."

"No." She snuggled in and rested her arm across his abdomen. "I'm fine. Better than fine, if I'm being honest. Finer than I've been in a long time."

"Me, too." He pulled the sheet up over them.

"It's a shame neither of us took pleasure in that at all," she said. "None. Zero."

"Yeah." That was probably the best pleasure he'd ever experienced, and for the life of him he couldn't explain why.

"For the record, my bed? Not proper. And it has to be said that proper is highly overrated."

"You and I have disagreed about many things, but that statement is not one of them."

Other than a nod, Tess didn't seem inclined to move, so Leo wasn't going to push it. Holding her felt too good after wanting her so badly for so long. Neither of them spoke, as if simply using their bodies to communicate contentment. He hadn't experienced it often in his life and savored the feeling now.

They might have dozed, because there was no telling how much time passed before Tess whispered, "Leo? Are you awake?"

"Yeah. You?"

She laughed and rubbed her cheek against his shoulder. "I've been thinking."

"I thought I smelled something burning."

"Very funny." She lightly tugged one of his chest hairs.

"Ow."

"Serves you right." She sighed then and the expression on her face was thoughtful. "I want to apologize."

"Why? That was awesome. Perfect." And he sincerely meant those words.

"I know. It really was." She didn't say anything for a few moments, as if choosing her words carefully. "I just want to say that I really misjudged you."

"What? How?"

"When my grandfather introduced us. The thing is, I'd heard about you, your reputation with women, and figured you were a cocky, arrogant player."

"A sports jerk like your ex." When she'd told him about that, he understood where she was coming from. "We've been through all this. It's water under the bridge. There's no reason to bring it up again."

"I just need to say this. Since we became partners, I've really gotten to know you."

"And I've gotten to know you. It's all good."

She looked up and met his gaze. "You're not an arrogant, cocky player at all. You are conscientious and caring. You're a really good man."

"Don't spread it around," he teased.

"I don't have to. Your actions speak louder than words. Working with the kids on the hockey team. Taking a personal interest in a troubled teenager. Being there for me. Talking me through my panic tonight. What would I have done without you?"

"Not a doubt in my mind that you would have moved forward and been just fine."

"Maybe. But it was fun experiencing the grand reopening of Patrick's Place with you. It was special because of you."

"It was special, but not because of me. You're the heart and soul of this place now," he said.

As partners went, she was the whole sexy package. Don't look now but he was successfully mixing business and pleasure with a woman who was as dead set against commitment as he was. How perfect was that? Contentment spilled over into happiness territory.

"I have to tell you something."

"You just did. And we're good."

"No, this is different," she insisted.

"Okay." But he looked at her shining eyes and suddenly got a very bad feeling. "What?"

"I'm in love with you, Leo."

Chapter Fourteen

Leo knew his reaction to Tess's declaration was going to be bad but that didn't begin to describe how much worse everything was from what he'd expected. First of all the words *I love you* almost came out of his mouth, too. Fortunately he stopped just in time. Things between them were pretty damn good, and the last thing he wanted was to screw it up with a responding emotional statement. But she'd put it out there. Now what was he supposed to say?

Why in God's name had he let her touch him? To feel the baby move. Damn it.

"Leo?" She sat up in the bed and held the sheet up to cover her breasts. "I'm sorry. The words just popped out. I didn't mean it."

Really? So she said that to every guy she slept with? He experienced an unexpected and uncomfortable spurt of jealousy at the thought of her with another guy. Good God. This was crazy and he was insane. Except she didn't sleep around—or so she'd told him. Could he believe her? A woman he thought he knew had lied to him before. He hated that but never more than he did right this minute. Destroying his ability to trust was the worst kind of betrayal.

And he couldn't think of any good response to Tess's words. So he simply said, "Don't worry about it."

"Can't help it. You look weird." She was staring at him. "Let's just pretend I never said those words."

"Done." He smiled at her but it was forced. The worry darkening her eyes told him she wasn't buying his answer. "Now you look weird."

"I wish I could take it back."

Unfortunately he couldn't unhear the words any more than he could undo getting her pregnant the first time they had sex in this building. He almost smiled remembering what she'd told him then. Saying it back to her now was worth a try.

"It never happened," he told her.

"Okay."

"We will never speak of this again." Her words, but life hadn't cooperated then, he thought.

Tess nodded but there was a sadness in her expression that ripped his heart out. He needed to get back on solid ground, back to the business, and their partnership was the way to do that. "The grand opening of Patrick's Place tonight was even better than I had hoped. Pat would be proud of you."

"Would he?" She was naked under that sheet and her hair was post-sex messy. "I'm not so sure."

She was making this personal. He couldn't really blame her. That tendency was hardwired into women. But he couldn't get sucked in. Trusting unconditionally once before had set him up to be knocked flat. The only thing that got him up again was the vow forged by fire in his soul, to never care that deeply again. And he was on the verge of breaking that vow. If she kept looking at him that way, with her eyes all soft and sexy, he was going to cave.

"It's late," he said. "And I have an early meeting tomorrow."

"Yeah. You should go."

Leo wasn't going to wait for her to say it again. He slid out of bed and quickly dressed. She didn't move and he had the uneasy feeling that if he touched her, she would shatter.

But he couldn't stop himself from kissing her on the forehead. "I'll lock the place up on my way out. You get some rest."

"Don't worry about me."

He couldn't help it but didn't say that out loud. "Good night, Tess."

He left before she could respond, urgently needing distance to take a deep breath. Hit the pause button and find a way to protect himself. Words meant nothing unless they were in writing.

Tess had never in her life regretted having a big mouth more than she did that night when she'd told Leo she loved him. Just because she felt it didn't mean she had to say the words out loud. It was just that the feeling was so big, she couldn't hold it back. Unfortunately he had looked as if he'd swallowed a bee and it was stinging all the way down.

And it wasn't as if it was entirely her fault. Their all business, no pleasure vow had exploded when he had kissed her. The problem was that her announcement about being in love with him had taken things to another level of awful.

The worst part was she hadn't seen him since that night a week ago. They'd texted, mostly about business. She'd reminded him of her upcoming doctor's appointment but he claimed he had a meeting. It hurt that he wasn't even giving her an opportunity to show him she could ignore what she'd said, to repair the damage she'd done to their business relationship.

It was late in more ways than one. The bar was nearing closing time, and Brandon was wiping down and tidying things while a few customers finished up their drinks. The dining area was closed and shut down, with the lights dimmed.

One of the last-call customers was John Alexander, the man who'd noticed she was pregnant and jumped to the correct conclusion that Leo was the father. In the last week, she'd had a lot of time to wonder if the older man's observations of her romantic feelings for Leo had compelled her to put the words out there. Not that she blamed John. The colossal error in judgment had been hers alone.

But she hadn't gone out of her way to speak to him tonight, so a case could be made that part of her did hold him responsible, and that wasn't fair. She was behind the bar and walked over to stand in front of him.

"Hi, John."

"Hey, Tess. How are you?"

"Good." It wasn't a complete lie because in time she would make things good again. She'd prove to Leo that she was trustworthy. "How about you? Doing okay?"

"Oh, you know." He toyed with the half-empty beer glass. "The missing her never really goes away."

The "her" he meant was his wife, and that meant he was still in love with her after all this time. Not what Tess wanted to hear. It wouldn't be that way for her; she wouldn't have to miss Leo, because he would come around. And what was so wrong with saying she loved him? A lot of people actually *wanted* to hear those words. But now she knew his story, knew he believed love brought pain and loss. Somehow she would convince him it wouldn't be that way with her.

She looked at the older man. "Do you wish you'd never fallen in love?"

"No. I wouldn't trade missing her now for never having loved her. Not in a million years." He met her gaze and his own was sad, although surprisingly peaceful. "She was the best thing that ever happened to me. She gave me the most precious gift of all. Our children."

"That's beautiful." She blinked at the tears stinging her eyes. Then she felt her baby move and pressed a hand to her abdomen. "Children are a blessing."

"True enough." He took a swallow of beer and stood. "It was last call a while ago and I'm sure Brandon wants to close up."

"Yeah."

"And you need your rest, young lady." He pretended to be stern but the twinkle in his eyes gave him away. Then he grew serious again. "Don't worry, honey. Whatever's going on with you and Leo will work itself out. Just wait and see. Things will be fine."

"How did you know there's something going on?" She shook her head. "I think you're psychic."

"Just observant. And only with people I care about." He smiled fondly. "Good night, Tess."

"See you soon."

A little while later everyone was gone, including Brandon. She was about to lock up when a familiar car pulled into the lot and parked outside Patrick's Place. Leo got out and walked to the front door, which she then opened.

He was literally a sight for sore eyes. As much as she'd told herself not to, she'd shed a few tears over him. And why did he have to look so darn handsome? So masculine. His worn jeans with that white cotton shirt, long sleeves rolled to mid-forearm, made her heart flutter. And she knew how the muscles under those clothes felt to the touch.

She could hardly breathe, but managed to say, "Hi."

"Sorry to show up so late."

"No problem." She hadn't expected him to show up at

all and wanted to say how happy she was. But she didn't want to compound her last mistake, so she kept the words bottled up. "Come on in."

He walked past her. "You probably want to get out of here and relax, so I won't keep you long."

"Actually I was going to look over today's receipts. What's up?"

"A couple of things. I have some papers from the lawyer and I had a meeting today with my accountant about Patrick's Place."

"And?" Side by side they walked over to the bar and she sat on one of the stools.

Leo set his briefcase on the chair next to hers, then met her gaze. "The accountant did revenue comparisons."

"Don't keep me in suspense. What did he say?"

"We're up 10 percent over last year, and business has currently increased by a lot—even when he backed out the numbers from the night of the opening." He smiled but it was surprisingly tense. "The bottom line is better than he'd hoped but he still cautioned that it's early. No high-fiving just yet."

She was working in the trenches, so to speak, and knew foot traffic was heavy. But it was a relief to have the numbers confirm her feelings. "That's fantastic."

"Yeah."

And yet his expression didn't match the sentiment. "So why do you look like someone just used your hockey stick for kindling?"

"For starters, I don't think a hockey stick is a good way to start a fire. They're made of fiberglass as a composite with wood, graphite or Kevlar. I'm not sure it would burn."

She didn't need to know that. He was procrastinating. What did he not want to tell her? "What's wrong, Leo?"

"Nothing's wrong. It's just… I have papers."

Probably some rider had kicked in from the partnership papers they'd originally signed. "From the lawyer, you said."

"Right." He pulled a manila folder out of his briefcase, set it on the bar and slid it closer to her.

Tess pulled out several long sheets of paper with dense legal paragraphs and glanced at the top—Custody Agreement and Child Support. She went ice-cold. "What is this?"

"I had Annabel draw it up. It spells out a joint-custody arrangement, if I'm the baby's father. And there's generous child support specified, too."

Since she told him he was going to be a father, he'd been okay with waiting until the baby was born to get DNA results and work things out then. Now he'd gone to his attorney to get papers drawn up for her to sign? "All of a sudden you need something carved in stone?"

"It's my bad. I should have done this right away."

"But you didn't. And the only thing that has changed is I told you I love you."

He shook his head. "This is about protecting the baby."

"Really? Come on, Leo."

"There's no other reason."

"If you truly believe that, you're burying your head in the sand." She refused to look away. "This is about me saying I love you."

"No—"

"Oh, please. It couldn't be any more clear unless you put up a barbed-wire fence to keep me out. You think my signing a piece of paper will prevent you from getting your heart broken again."

"You're wrong." His tone was hard and his expression grim.

"Am I?" She knew she wasn't but he needed to hear this. "Everything was fine and dandy until I had the audacity to tell you how I feel. Now you have a legal document for my signature. What would you think?"

"It's my goal to protect everyone. To have everything spelled out in black-and-white. If the baby is mine—"

"I'm going to say this one more time. The baby is yours. And if you believe I would keep your child from you, you don't know me at all. Every child deserves to know their parents. So you just wasted a lot of money on a lawyer and an agreement you really don't need."

She slid off the stool and walked around behind the bar, where there were pens for signing credit card receipts. When she found one, she looked him straight in the eye before scratching her signature on the line where indicated.

"There. Just so you know, I signed this because I know you're afraid. I hope it gives you peace of mind."

"Tess, I—"

"No. There's nothing more to say." She started toward the hall and the stairs leading up to her apartment. Then she stopped. There was one more thing and he wasn't going to like this either, but how much more paperwork could a lawyer draw up to protect him? She turned back and said, "I'm not her, Leo. I'm not going to lie and cheat. I think you know that. And you're a fool if you walk away from what we have together. But I think you know that, too—"

Emotion choked off her words and she turned away to hurry upstairs. Every time he saw her cry she ended up in his arms. He made it clear he couldn't love her. She could read between the lines of that damn legal agreement. So there was no way she would let him see her cry. Not again.

* * *

When Tess signed that stupid agreement with tears glistening in her eyes, Leo knew he'd royally screwed up. It wasn't the tears that had convinced him, but the way he wanted to kick himself into next year for hurting her. Then he had ached to hold her and make it better, but she had walked away before he could.

He couldn't blame her. She'd nailed it when she accused him of being afraid. He wanted nothing to do with love, but he cared about her. There was no reason to put a label on it. Thinking about it had kept him awake a lot for the better part of last week, and he'd come to the conclusion that she was right about everything. He didn't believe she would lie and cheat. For several days he'd been trying to tell her that, but she was giving him the cold shoulder every time he came into Patrick's Place.

Now he was here to try again. He parked in the lot and walked inside, then looked around. Finally he spotted her behind the bar, drawing a beer. It was happy hour but he wasn't feeling especially happy. She was smiling when she set the frosty glass on a napkin in front of a customer. Leo really liked her smile and missed it aimed in his direction.

"'Winners never quit. Quitters never win,'" he muttered to himself as he headed in her direction.

He sat down at her end of the bar. Brandon was on the far side, pouring liquor into a shot glass for a cocktail, then adding a lot of olives. He delivered the drink to a very attractive twentysomething blonde who smiled and flirted with the young man. Being a bartender had its perks. Being a bar owner who was getting the cold shoulder from his partner did not. It was time to make things right between them.

Tess had her back to him, washing glasses and wiping

down counters. When she turned, he noticed that the pregnancy was really showing. There was no way she could conceal it now. And she looked more beautiful than he'd ever seen her. Glowing even.

Until she focused on him and her expression hardened into ice.

"Tess—"

"Do you want a drink?"

No. He wanted to talk to her but he had a feeling ordering something was the only way to make that happen. "Yeah. Can I get a beer?"

Without a word she moved to get him a frosty glass, then held it beneath the tap and pulled the handle. She tilted the glass to keep the foam to a minimum, then leveled it at just the right moment. She grabbed a napkin and set it on the bar, in front of him, with the glass on top.

"Thanks. How are you?"

"Fine." She was treating him like a stranger.

That wasn't actually true. A stranger who came in for a beer would get a warm smile and an enthusiastic welcome to Patrick's Place. He longed to be a stranger.

"I'm sorry I missed the doctor's appointment. There was a crisis. Pipe broke in one of my buildings. Is everything all right with you and the baby?"

"I'll let you know after the birth, when the DNA test results are in. According to our legal agreement, that's when it will be okay for you to start feeling anything."

"Come on, Tess. Can't we talk about this?"

"Call your attorney. Get her to draw up more paperwork. I'll look at it."

Before he could come up with a response, she walked away. She stopped to talk to Brandon, who nodded, and then she left the bar and went upstairs to her apartment.

"That went well." Now he was talking to himself.

He would keep talking if he had any helpful advice to give to himself, but that well was dry. Everything he'd tried so far wasn't working. So maybe he needed to talk to someone else. Tess's sarcastic comment was still ringing in his ears. *Call your attorney.* Annabel did legal work for him but was also a friend. So that was actually a very good idea.

He took out his phone and looked through his contacts. She was probably still in the office. It went straight to voice mail, so he texted her a brief message. 9-1-1. His phone rang moments later.

He answered and said, "Annabel—"

"What's wrong?"

"I need to talk," he said.

"Is this a legal matter?"

"Sort of." It was a result of the document she'd pulled together for him. "Are you with a client?"

"Nope. No more appointments. I'm at the office, catching up on paperwork."

"Can I come over?" he asked.

There was a brief pause before she said, "Okay."

He clicked off and headed for the door. There were four guys sitting in a booth and one of them called him over.

The man was balding, in his fifties. "Aren't you Leo 'The Wall' Wallace? The hockey player?"

"Yes, but—"

"Can we get your autograph?" He lifted his beer from the cocktail napkin and pulled a pen from his shirt pocket.

"Sure." Leo signed his name and handed it back.

"How's retirement?" one of the other men asked. "Do you miss playing? Games? Glory? Girls?"

He thought about the question and realized he hadn't missed those days for a long time. Life was filled with work. And Tess. She had brought joy and purpose to him, to his life. And soon there would be a baby. His baby.

"Everything I want is right here." Except Tess. He glanced at the four men. "Sorry to cut this short, but I have a meeting. Hope you'll come back in. I'd love to chat with you."

Everyone smiled and assured him he could count on their business. He waved on his way out the door and twenty minutes later he walked into the building where Annabel's office was located. He took the elevator to her floor and when it stopped, he headed down the hall. The receptionist was gone so he walked into the inner sanctum, where Annabel sat behind her desk.

"Where's the fire?" She didn't bother with pleasantries.

For some reason that irked him. "Hello, Annabel. How are you?"

"Annoyed. That's how I am. You said this was an emergency. To me that means someone—you—is either bleeding or on fire. If you are, it doesn't show."

That's because it was all happening to him on the inside. "I needed to talk."

"You could have called the office tomorrow and made an appointment."

"Since when do friends have to put a date on the calendar to talk?"

"So, we're friends."

"Of course we are. You know that." He felt like a lawyer presenting an argument in court. "I need to talk to you about something. You're logical and you're a woman."

"Oh, boy." She sighed and put down her pen. "This isn't going to be quick, is it?"

"No."

"Okay."

He counted on his friend's professional advice and

knew she would give him the truth. Always. They never mixed business and pleasure. But he'd crossed that line with Tess. Touching her made his willpower evaporate and he'd kissed her. He was a goner. And then she'd said what she'd said, and he ran for cover. He had to make things better, and not just so they could work together.

"Sorry. I'll buy you dinner later."

"Maybe. If I'm still hungry after you're finished confessing how you've been a jackass. After which I will give you outstanding advice on how to make up for your insensitive behavior."

"Wow. That's harsh," he said.

"Tell me I'm wrong."

"After you tell me how you know this." He sat in one of the club chairs in front of her desk.

"Seriously?" She sighed when he nodded. "I drew up that completely unnecessary agreement for you after you insisted you had to have it."

"How do you know it's unnecessary?"

"First of all I've met Tess. I like her and I'm an excellent judge of character. She is sweet, honest and oozing integrity."

Leo could not argue with that assessment. And she was so much more, too. Hot, sexy and smart. Prettiest pregnant lady he'd ever seen. She kept him on his toes. "What else?"

"How do you know there's more?"

"You said 'first of all.' That implies you have more criteria for your conclusion."

"Okay. Yeah." Annabel leaned back in her chair. "You had a verbal agreement with Tess to have DNA testing done after the baby is born. So there was no reason to have anything in writing right now." She met his gaze and frowned. "Unless something happened. Is Tess okay? The baby?"

"Both fine." At least that's what she'd said.

"For some reason you felt threatened. Because everything in those papers was about your rights being protected." Her eyes widened in comprehension. "She told you she has feelings for you, didn't she?"

Leo considered lying but there was no point. Besides, he'd 9-1-1-ed her and rushed over here to talk. "Yes. She said she loved me."

"Great." She looked pleased, then studied his face. "Or not."

"Come on. You know what happened to me. I fell in love, got lied to and lost my kid. If I hadn't fallen for her…" He shook his head. "Love is the last thing I want."

"Tess isn't your ex." Leave it to a lawyer to state the obvious.

"That's what she said."

"And letting her go because of your personal baggage makes you an idiot."

"She said that, too. Only she called me a fool."

"That works." Annabel glanced away for a moment, then met his gaze. Her own was intense. "A fool who's taken one too many shots to the head playing hockey."

"What does that mean?" He held up a hand. "I don't mean that literally. Why in the world would I take another chance in my personal life after what happened to me?"

"Because by some miracle of banked karma, you knocked up a really wonderful woman who is the one for you. God knows why, but she genuinely cares about you. And you made her sign something that proves you don't trust her."

It sounded really bad when she put it like that. "I guess I could have handled it better."

"You think?" Annabel gave him her patented "men are morons" look.

"Okay. Already established. Asked and answered, as you lawyers like to say. What do I do? How do I fix this with her?"

"Did it occur to you to say you're sorry?"

"Of course. I tried. I've *been* trying ever since I messed up."

"Not going well." Again stating the obvious. It sure looked as if she was taking a whole lot of satisfaction from that.

"If it was all sunshine and roses, I wouldn't have called you. Are you going to keep making fun of me? Or are you actually going to give me some common-sense suggestions to fix this problem?"

"Poor Leo." She tsked and her expression was a little condescending. "I'm sorry you're hurting. Truly. I just couldn't resist."

"Try harder. Tell me what to do."

"You, sir, need a very big gesture. Flowers. Jewelry is always nice. Expensive. A conciliatory billboard on Huntington Hills Parkway."

"That's the most congested intersection in town," he said.

"Like I said—very big gesture. Very public, too. Followed by a great deal of sincere groveling," she added.

"I was afraid you were going to say that."

"Telling her you were wrong will work wonders. You'll see. I promise."

"How can you be so sure I'm going to do this?"

She smiled now, a look without a hint of sarcasm or female satisfaction over a man's confusion. This was sincere and heartfelt. "I know you will because you're crazy about her."

At least she hadn't used the *L* word, but it was sounding pretty good to him. And she obviously knew him well. Because he was going back to the bar and this time he was going to make Tess listen.

Chapter Fifteen

When Tess heard the knock on her apartment door her heart jumped. Maybe Leo had followed her. But when she opened up and saw her friend Carla, she realized the word *maybe* was the cruelest, most painful one in the English language.

She forced herself to smile and hugged the other woman. "Hi."

"Hi, back." Carla held her at arm's length, studying her. "I was going to ask how you are, but you look tired. Are you eating? Sleeping? Taking care of yourself?"

"Of course." She shut the door. "To what do I owe this unexpected visit?"

"I haven't heard from you in an uncharacteristically long time." She shrugged. "They don't call. They don't write. They don't—"

"You've made your point. I've been busy with work."

"Aren't we all," Carla said wryly.

"So you came by yourself. Where's Jamie?"

"Bill is back in town." Carla had a look on her face, as if she'd eaten bad sushi. "She sends her love and made me promise to give her an update."

"What's wrong?" Tess asked. It was a relief to be talking about someone other than herself.

"I don't know how to tell her, but I think Bill is a two-timing, scum-sucking, cheating bastard."

"What are you talking about?" Tess asked.

"I'm pretty sure he's married."

Tess pointed to the kitchen. "Can I get you a glass of wine?"

"Sure. I could really use one."

Tess led the way and took a bottle of white wine from the refrigerator that she kept chilled for her friends and opened it. Reaching up into the cupboard, she took down a stemless glass and poured the golden liquid into it, then handed it over. She took out a bottle of water for herself.

"What makes you think he's married?"

"The signs are classic. He shows up unexpectedly and she has to drop everything to see him. The pub reopened and he's suddenly called back to the home office. And yes, I do mean that as a double entendre. She suggested the two of them take a romantic getaway to San Diego, but he wouldn't hear of it." Carla took a big drink of wine. "I just have a feeling and I don't want her to get hurt. But I'm afraid if I say something, she'll be mad at me."

"If he is, she's going to be hurt anyway. Wouldn't it be best to gently ask some questions? Maybe lead her in that direction without actually putting it out there?"

Carla nodded. "That's a good idea. It would help if you're there when I bring it up."

"Count on it." Tess hated to see her friend hurt, especially because she knew how bad it felt. The best thing she could say was that Leo hadn't lied to her, probably because he'd been lied to so horribly. She wanted to change the subject. "So, what's new? How's the matchmaking business?"

"Things are looking up since Gabriel Blackburne is temporarily helping out his eccentric aunt, who owns Make Me a Match."

"Isn't he in the tech business?"

"Yes, but the place desperately needed organization. Lillian is emotional and intuitive, super good at pairing people. He's analytical and brings balance." Carla took another sip of her wine. "It's amazing how many people would like to find someone but are too busy to look."

Tess hadn't been looking. It had just happened, damn it. Everything led back to Leo. She saw that Carla's wineglass was empty. "Can I refill that for you?"

"Since you're pregnant and can't have alcohol, does that mean I'm drinking for two?"

"Whatever you want. And you don't have to drive home. You can spend the night here."

Carla's eyes widened questioningly. "I suppose that means there's no chance you're going to have male companionship this evening."

"Why would you think that?"

"I saw the way you were looking at him when Patrick's Place reopened," Carla said.

"Are you talking about Leo?"

"Is there someone else I don't know about?"

Tess hadn't talked to her friends about the agreement he'd had drawn up for her to sign. Was there such a thing as being too heartbroken to even discuss it with the people you trusted most in the world? She'd been trying to pretend things were fine. The "never speak of it again" solution to her pain was working, just barely. And she wanted to keep it that way.

"Honestly, you don't even know about Leo."

"What don't I know?" Carla took the refilled glass.

"There's not much to know," she insisted.

"Well, I know you and your eyes are telling me that there's a lot on your mind. My matchmaking instincts are telling me it's all about one hunky hockey-player partner of yours."

"How long have you been working at this new job?" Tess asked.

"That's irrelevant." Carla waved a hand in dismissal.

"A couple of months gives you a matchmaking sixth sense?"

"Are you ever going to let me forget that before I hated him for hurting you, I actually liked Alan, the college athlete and first-class jerk?"

"I'm so over that." But Tess had a bad feeling that getting over Leo was going to be a lifetime struggle.

"We've known each other how long?" Carla asked. "Do you seriously think I can't see that something is up? If the shoe was on the other foot, would you not badger me until I came clean?"

"God, I hate it when you're right." Tess sighed. "Leo and I slept together."

"Old news, sweetie." Carla's gaze dropped to Tess's growing baby bump. "You're the cutest darn pregnant lady I've ever seen."

That made Tess smile. Thank goodness for her friends. She was being stupid by keeping this to herself. They'd helped her through every crisis, and this one would be no exception, because shutting them out wasn't an option. It would not be allowed.

"Let's sit," she said.

"Are you uncomfortable?" Carla looked concerned.

"A little. Feeling some pressure but that happens if I'm on my feet a lot. It goes away when I sit."

"Okay, then." Her friend moved to the love seat that separated the living area and kitchen. "Take a load off right now, missy."

Tess did just that and sighed before meeting the other woman's gaze. "The thing is, we had sex again, about a week ago, and—"

"I knew it! Like I said, off-the-chart chemistry between you two that night." There was an "I told you so" gleam in Carla's eyes. "Jamie and I talked about it on the way home and she saw it, too. My matchmaking mojo was crackling when I saw the way he was looking at you." She took a breath, then a sip of wine. "How did he propose? Was it romantic? Rose petals and champagne—well, not for you. But knowing you as I do, you're going to make love complicated because of the past. Please tell me you didn't turn him down flat."

"Things are definitely complicated, but not because of me." Tess held up her left hand and pointed out the bare ring finger. "He didn't propose."

"What's he waiting for? The two of you are clearly nuts about each other."

Nuts described Tess. She'd been deluded enough to fall for the guy, even though she knew it was a really bad idea. But that implied she'd had a choice. It had just happened. She hadn't wanted to lose her heart. Tears filled her eyes and that's why she'd resisted talking about this. But no way would her friend let this pass without hearing details.

"Tell me, Tess. What's wrong? Was it the sex? Bad?"

"No. It was really, really awesome. And I don't care if that word is overused." She sniffled. "And I was so in the moment. And the feeling was so big, it spilled over and—"

"What?" Carla demanded.

"I said it. I told him I love him."

"But that's a good thing, right? Tell me it is. For the sake of my career in bringing people together to find happiness. Which isn't easy, by the way." Carla looked worried. "Did he say it back?"

Tess shook her head. "He had his lawyer draw up an agreement for joint custody and child support *if* DNA proves the baby is his. He doesn't trust me, and that makes love impossible."

"But why? How could he not believe in you? You're the most honorable person I know. Besides Jamie, of course. What's wrong with him?"

"He wants no part of love." A tear trickled down Tess's cheek.

"Coldhearted jerk." Carla's eyes blazed and angry red blotches covered the fair skin of her face. "I'm going to hurt him—"

"No. He has a very good reason for feeling that way." Tess told her friend everything. "He never promised to love me and hasn't done anything wrong. The mistake is mine."

"Well, that really bites. And I can't even be mad at him." Carla put her glass on the coffee table, then reached over and squeezed Tess's hand. "What can I do?"

"Same as you always have. Be my friend." That did it. The sobs she'd been holding in fought their way out as tears spilled down her cheeks. She buried her face in her hands and let all the pain come out while her friend held her.

"It will be okay, honey. I promise. You're not alone. Not ever."

Tess had no idea how long the storm lasted but eventually there were no more tears left to shed. No offense to her friend, but it was a lot more comforting when Leo held her while she cried. Guess that was over, too.

She brushed the wetness from her cheeks and tried to smile. "Sorry about that."

"Don't be silly. You should have told me sooner, you know."

"Yeah." Tess nodded. "But it was hard. I hope you never have your heart broken, but if you do, I'll return the favor and hold you while you cry."

"Are you kidding? I'm never going to fall in love ever again."

"Yeah, that's what I said. Famous last words. And isn't that attitude a violation of the matchmaker code of conduct?"

"The business is about facilitating meetings for people who are looking for someone. The love part is up to them. Or not. My background in psychology is helpful. From reading profiles, it's a tool in pairing up people, but there's no way to predict what happens face-to-face. It's a job and I needed one badly after what happened with you know who."

"Good for you moving past all that. I'm glad I don't have to worry about you being an idiot, like me—" Her voice broke. "Damn hormones."

"Go into the bathroom and wash your face," Carla ordered. "Put a cold compress on your eyes. That was an ugly cry. You'll feel much better. No argument. Go."

Tess did as instructed and went to the bathroom right off her bedroom. She splashed cold water on her face, then wet a cloth and wrung it out before pressing it to her eyes. It did make her feel better. After a while she started to feel guilty about leaving her friend alone for so long. But before she went back out, it would be prudent to use the facilities.

When she sat, something on her panties caught her eye and she gasped. "Oh, God—"

There was a knock on the door, followed by Carla's voice. "Are you okay in there?"

"I'm bleeding, Carla. The baby…"

Leo left his lawyer's office and went straight back to Patrick's Place. Annabel had obviously gotten through to him pretty fast because the four hockey fanboys were still sitting in the same booth. He waved to them on his way past. Another time he would chat them up, but he was a man on a mission. He needed to find Tess ASAP.

He scanned the crowded bar area, the filled-to-capacity lounge, where a baseball game was on, and then the dining area. There was no sign of her. To get a better look, he walked closer, making sure he hadn't missed any corner. He hadn't and was surprised she wasn't here. Every night she poured drinks or visited with customers and worked harder than anyone. Because this investment was personal and emotional for her.

It was possible she was still avoiding him, but she wouldn't do that at the expense of her business.

"Brandon." He stepped up to the bar, where the young man was standing.

"Hey, Leo. I thought you were gone. It's been a busy night. I think you'll really be happy when you see the—"

He held up a hand. Wow. Did everyone think he was only about business? "Take a breath. I'm not here to check up on you."

"Okay." He smiled a little sheepishly. "How are you?"

"Been better. Is Tess around?"

"I haven't seen her for a while. Come to think of it, the last time I saw her was when you were in here before. I think she went upstairs then."

"She didn't tell you she was taking the rest of the night off?"

"No."

Leo knew she would have so she must be in her apartment. "Thanks, Brandon. By the way, you're doing a great job and when we open the second location of Patrick's Place, you're my first choice to manage it."

"We're expanding?"

"If things keep going the way they are—yes."

Brandon smiled broadly. "That's great news."

"See you later. I'm going to talk to Tess now."

"Okay, boss."

Leo headed for the hall and took the stairs two at a time. He knocked on the door and moments later it was opened. By Tess's friend Carla.

He smiled at her. "Hi—"

"Leo, thank God." She pulled him inside and was surprisingly strong for a small woman.

"What's up?"

"It's Tess."

The woman was clearly shaken, and fear sliced through him. "Where is she?"

"In the bedroom. I—"

He didn't wait for the rest and hurried past her. Tess was stretched out on the bed with her eyes closed. She looked small, fragile and tense. He moved closer and said, "Tess, what's wrong?"

Her eyes popped open. "Leo, I'm bleeding. It shouldn't be happening—"

"Okay." The fear got bigger but he forced calm into his voice.

"Carla made me lie down."

"Good." He knelt beside the bed. "But I think you should be looked at."

"I'll wait and see if it stops. I'll call the doctor—"

"Carla can do that and let her know you're at the emergency room."

"What are you saying?"

"I'm taking you to the hospital. Now."

She caught her top lip between her teeth and then nodded. "I'll get up and—"

"No." He stood, then scooped her into his arms as

gently as possible. "I'll try not to jostle you too much but this is the fastest way."

She was scared. He knew that because she didn't protest. He really, really wished she was arguing with him right now.

He met her gaze and tried to look more reassuring than he felt. For her sake. And the baby's. *His* baby. "Here we go. You ready?"

"Yes." She put her arms around his neck and hung on.

He carried her through the apartment, and Tess told her friend where to find the doctor's number and to call the answering service right away. Leo asked her to let Brandon know he was closing up tonight. He didn't want Tess to worry about it.

At the car he set her on her feet in order to fish the keys out of his pocket, hit the fob to unlock the doors and then opened the passenger side.

When he started to lift her again she said, "I can handle this."

Five minutes later they were at the hospital's emergency entrance, and he found a parking space close to the automatic doors. This time he ignored her protest that she could walk and carried her inside to the check-in desk. The staff got her into an exam room right away, then shooed him into the hall while they got her hooked up to monitors.

The door opened again and he was allowed back in. Tess was in a patient gown and the machines were rhythmically beeping. He was going to believe the sounds meant all was perfectly normal. She was still pale and scared, but looked a little calmer.

Leo pulled a chair over and sat. "What did they say?"

"Nothing. I'm waiting for the doctor. She's here for a

delivery. Isn't that lucky?" Her mouth trembled and her eyes filled with tears. "I'm so scared. My baby—"

"It's okay. Everything is going to be fine."

"Is it? You don't know that."

"You have to believe, Tess."

"Really? How can you even say that to me with a straight face?" With shaking hands she brushed the wetness from her cheeks. "You've never believed this baby was yours."

"It's mine," he said firmly.

"You don't have to say that because I'm in the ER. Don't you dare feel sorry for me."

"Nothing could be further from the truth." He took her hand and held it in both of his. "And you're wrong. I believed from the beginning that this is my baby."

"Oh, please."

"It's the truth," he insisted. "Deep down I knew it because Patrick Morrow's granddaughter was raised to be scrupulously honest. But after what I went through, I was trying to protect myself and denial was the best I could do."

Her face softened. "Then why make me sign those papers?"

"You said you love me and I went into survival mode again. Fight-or-flight."

"Then you get a gold star for that. Because you did both at the same time. An awesome multitasker." There was a little sass back in her voice.

"That's me. Overachiever at the worst time."

"Why worst?" she asked.

"It's the last thing I should have done. Because I love you."

"You have a very funny way of showing it," she scoffed.

"What can I say? Lack of a positive male role model. Except your grandfather. He showed me what love looks like."

"Me, too," she said sadly.

Leo nodded. "I have a sneaking suspicion that he was pushing us together."

"What?"

"He knew a lot of people who could have invested money in his business but he picked me. I think somehow he knew I was in love with you even then."

"He picked you because…" She stopped when his words sank in. "What? Are you really saying you love me?"

"I fell in love with you the first time I saw you."

She looked skeptical and had every right. "That's a very romantic thing to say. But—"

He put a finger to her lips to stop the words. "No *buts*. It's the truth and everything is going to be okay. We'll get through this together."

"Men always say that but don't mean it."

"I promise I mean it."

The door opened then and Dr. Thompson came in. She was wearing blue scrubs and a white lab coat. He felt better that she was here even though she threw him out of the room to examine Tess.

Leo paced the hall like a caged tiger. Or expectant father. It felt like a lifetime before the doctor let him back in. She was very reassuring and told them it wasn't unusual for spotting to occur. But she had no doubt that the baby was absolutely fine. Tess was to stay off her feet and take it easy for a few days, and Leo intended to see that she followed the doctor's orders.

After she was discharged, he drove her home and insisted she go straight to bed. Then he fixed her something light to eat and made sure she ate it.

"Is there anything else you need?" he asked.

"No." She smiled. "Thanks for everything. You should go home and get some rest. You must be tired."

"I'm not. And I'm not leaving." He sat in the chair near the bed and put his long legs up on the ottoman.

"What are you doing?"

"I told you we're going to get through this together. I'm settling in for the night."

"Why?"

"Clearly I have my work cut out for me to prove that I mean what I say. But I will prove it. And after I do, I'll convince you to marry me."

A sweet smile curved the corners of her beautiful mouth before she sat up in the bed. "Yes."

"Yes, what?"

"Yes, I'll marry you." She patted the empty space beside her in the bed. "Because, as you know, I love you. Very much. And I would never let my fiancé sleep in a chair."

Happiness and relief poured through him as he slid in beside her. He pulled her into his arms and kissed her gently. "This was the worst and best day of my life."

"Oh?"

"Our baby is fine. You love me. And we're getting married. A personal hat trick."

"I love it when you talk hockey to me." She snuggled close and rested her cheek on his chest. "And now you can do it for the rest of our lives."

That was the game plan.

Epilogue

Tess stood in the doorway of the baby's nursery and watched Leo holding their little girl. Leonore Patricia Wallace. The sight of her handsome husband—Leo "The Wall" Wallace—so gentle and sweet with that tiny bundle of pink preciousness, was too *everything* for words. She pulled her cell phone from the pocket of her jeans and snapped a picture. This was something she'd done countless times in the month since she gave birth. And every single picture was priceless.

Leo looked away from the baby and smiled. "Hey, Mrs. Wallace."

"Hey, Mr. Wallace."

Her heart was so full of love for this man, she was afraid it might explode. Many times over he'd convinced her that he was there and they'd see things through together. He'd been the best coach ever during labor and delivery. He was her rock, her love, her heart. And she was his. She remembered when this house was barely furnished, but not anymore.

"I love this room," she said, looking around.

"Me, too."

They had chosen not to know the sex of the baby and had decorated in gender-neutral colors and theme. The walls were cream with white trim. Framed prints of animals—pudgy hippos, elephants and giraffes—were on the walls.

The chest of drawers that also served as a changing table was cherry wood, as was the crib. Not that Leonore would use it for a while, what with the cradle in the master bedroom. Both she and Leo wanted the baby in their room until she was bigger.

Tess came closer and studied the tiny girl peacefully sleeping in her father's arms. "I think she has your chin. I love that little indentation."

"Mine or hers?"

"Both."

"She definitely has my disposition," he said proudly. "Mellow and serene."

Tess couldn't make a comparison since this was her first baby. But Leo had been through this before, a seasoned pro at this whole infant thing. She was wondering how he was feeling about it.

"Are you okay?" she asked.

"Yes." He looked up at her and seemed to know what she was thinking. "I will always love Chad and hope that he's healthy and happy. That his parents are good to him and he grows up well. But the emptiness I had inside for so long was gone the day you married me."

"Yeah. That was a good day." As was every single one since.

Their wedding happened not long after the night he'd carried her into the emergency room. After that, he was in a hurry not to waste time, but would have waited if she'd wanted to do it after giving birth. Have the dress, reception—the whole nine yards. Tess didn't care about anything except him and their baby.

They'd closed Patrick's Place for a night, found a minister and taken vows in front of close friends. No family, at least not living and breathing relatives. She was convinced her grandfather was there, watching over them, happy that the two of them had been smart enough not to blow off his matchmaking efforts.

"Are you okay?" he asked.

The discomfort of birth had faded and she was tired, what with having a newborn and being up at night. But she'd never dreamed happiness this complete was possible.

"I'm so good, it's scary," she said. "I have everything I've always wanted. You. Our baby. A family."

"I feel the same way." The baby started squeaking and squirming, so he shifted her to his shoulder.

Sometimes Tess still felt awkward doing that, but he was confident and sure of himself. His big hands were exquisitely gentle with their tiny human.

He smiled up at her. "It occurs to me that we're rich in family."

"How do you mean?"

"Think about it. There's you, me and Leonore. Then we have our Patrick's Place regulars."

"Yeah." Her gaze slid to the stack of baby gifts still in the corner of the room from all of their customers. Sitting on top of the pile was a small pink helmet, a gift from Josh and all the guys on the team. "And we have our hockey family."

"Exactly." He stood when the baby started to fuss and handed her to Tess. "That's her hungry cry."

"How do you know the difference between that, the one when her diaper needs changing and the general one when she's bored and needs to be held?"

"It's a gift." He shrugged.

"You're going to make me look bad. If you had the right equipment I'm sure you would feed her, too."

"I would go to hell and back if it meant my daughter would be happy," he said.

She kissed the small cheek, then smiled at him. "You are the baby whisperer."

"I'm a very lucky man."

"You didn't feel that way when I first told you I was pregnant." She laughed, remembering that conversation. And everything that happened afterward. "Maybe we should have named our little peanut Cupid."

"Because she brought us together." He put his arm around her shoulders, hugging them both.

Because of how close they'd come to missing out on this happiness, Tess would always believe that her grandfather was watching over them. "We are very lucky."

"I couldn't agree more."

Tess had the traditional family she'd always wanted, and the dream had started in a nontraditional way. They'd gone from conflict to contentment all because of an unexpected partnership.

* * * * *

Look for Teresa Southwick's next book set in Huntington Hills in October 2019!

And in the meantime, try her Bachelors of Blackwater Lake miniseries, beginning with

Finding Family…and Forever?
One Night with the Boss
The Rancher Who Took Her In

Available now from Harlequin Special Edition!

COMING NEXT MONTH FROM

HARLEQUIN®

SPECIAL EDITION

Available April 16, 2019

#2689 A FORTUNATE ARRANGEMENT
The Fortunes of Texas: The Lost Fortunes
by Nancy Robards Thompson
After five years of working—and falling for—Austin Fortune, Felicity Schafer seems no closer to a promotion, or to getting Austin to open up. Will giving notice finally get Austin to *take* notice?

#2690 SWITCHED AT BIRTH
The Bravos of Valentine Bay • by Christine Rimmer
After finding out she was switched at birth, Madison Delaney heads to Valentine Bay to learn more about her birth family. She never expected to have feelings about Stren Larson, the shipbuilder who lives next door to her rental. But they come from such different worlds... Will they be able to see if those feelings can turn into forever?

#2691 HIS TEXAS RUNAWAY
Men of the West • by Stella Bagwell
Veterinarian Chandler Hollister has brought home many strays...but no one like lovely Roslyn DuBose. Exhausted, the single soon-to-be mom gratefully accepts his help. As one night becomes many days, Roslyn finds her way into Chandler's heart. But before this working man becomes a family man, Roslyn must face the one obstacle to their happy future: her secret past.

#2692 DOUBLE DUTY FOR THE COWBOY
Match Made in Haven • by Brenda Harlen
When Regan Channing finds herself pregnant, the last thing she expects is for another man to make her his wife! *Especially* not former bad boy Connor Neal. Pretty soon Regan's newborn twins have him wrapped around their fingers. But can the deputy's debt of obligation ever become true love?

#2693 THE CITY GIRL'S HOMECOMING
Furever Yours • by Kathy Douglass
Recent New York transplant Megan Jennings just found the ideal temporary home for sixteen suddenly displaced pets. Too bad the farm's owner isn't giving her the same warm welcome. A city girl broke Cade Battle's heart, and he refuses to trust the feelings Megan awakens. But Megan knows she's finally found her forever family. Can she make Cade believe it, too?

#2694 DEALMAKER, HEARTBREAKER
Wickham Falls Weddings • by Rochelle Alers
Big-city man Noah Wainwright has always viewed business as a game. But when he stumbles across bed-and-breakfast owner Viviana Remington, she's playing by different rules. Rules that bring the love-'em-and-leave-'em playboy to his knees... But when Viv learns how the Wainwright family plays the game, all bets are off.

YOU CAN FIND MORE INFORMATION ON UPCOMING HARLEQUIN® TITLES, FREE EXCERPTS AND MORE AT WWW.HARLEQUIN.COM.

HSECNM0419

Get 4 FREE REWARDS!

We'll send you 2 FREE Books plus 2 FREE Mystery Gifts.

Harlequin® Special Edition books feature heroines finding the balance between their work life and personal life on the way to finding true love.

FREE Value Over $20

YES! Please send me 2 FREE Harlequin® Special Edition novels and my 2 FREE gifts (gifts are worth about $10 retail). After receiving them, if I don't wish to receive any more books, I can return the shipping statement marked "cancel." If I don't cancel, I will receive 6 brand-new novels every month and be billed just $4.99 per book in the U.S. or $5.74 per book in Canada. That's a savings of at least 12% off the cover price! It's quite a bargain! Shipping and handling is just 50¢ per book in the U.S. and 75¢ per book in Canada.* I understand that accepting the 2 free books and gifts places me under no obligation to buy anything. I can always return a shipment and cancel at any time. The free books and gifts are mine to keep no matter what I decide.

235/335 HDN GMY2

Name (please print)

Address Apt. #

City State/Province Zip/Postal Code

Mail to the **Reader Service:**
IN U.S.A.: P.O. Box 1341, Buffalo, NY 14240-8531
IN CANADA: P.O. Box 603, Fort Erie, Ontario L2A 5X3

Want to try 2 free books from another series? Call 1-800-873-8635 or visit www.ReaderService.com.

*Terms and prices subject to change without notice. Prices do not include sales taxes, which will be charged (if applicable) based on your state or country of residence. Canadian residents will be charged applicable taxes. Offer not valid in Quebec. This offer is limited to one order per household. Books received may not be as shown. Not valid for current subscribers to Harlequin® Special Edition books. All orders subject to approval. Credit or debit balances in a customer's account(s) may be offset by any other outstanding balance owed by or to the customer. Please allow 4 to 6 weeks for delivery. Offer available while quantities last.

Your Privacy—The Reader Service is committed to protecting your privacy. Our Privacy Policy is available online at www.ReaderService.com or upon request from the Reader Service. We make a portion of our mailing list available to reputable third parties that offer products we believe may interest you. If you prefer that we not exchange your name with third parties, or if you wish to clarify or modify your communication preferences, please visit us at www.ReaderService.com/consumerschoice or write to us at Reader Service Preference Service, P.O. Box 9062, Buffalo, NY 14240-9062. Include your complete name and address.

HSE19R

SPECIAL EXCERPT FROM

HARLEQUIN™

SPECIAL EDITION

Big-city man Noah Wainwright has always viewed business as a game. When he stumbles across bed-and-breakfast owner Viviana Remington, she's playing by different rules. Rules that bring the love-'em-and-leave-'em playboy to his knees... But when Viv learns how the Wainwright family plays the game, all bets are off.

Read on for a sneak preview of Dealmaker, Heartbreaker, *the next great book in bestselling author Rochelle Alers's Wickham Falls Weddings miniseries.*

After the walk on the beach, she'd become overly polite and distant. Knowing he wasn't going to sleep, Noah sat up and tossed back the sheets. He found a pair of shorts and slipped them on. Barefoot, he unlocked the screen door and walked out into the night. He saw something out of the corner of his eye and spied someone sitting on the beach. A full moon lit up the night, and as he made his way down to the water, he couldn't stop smiling.

She glanced up at him and smiled. "It looks as if I'm not the only one who couldn't sleep."

Noah sank down next to her on the damp sand. Even in the eerie light, he could discern that the sun had darkened her skin to a deep mahogany. "I was never much of an insomniac before meeting you."

Viviana pulled her legs up to her chest and wrapped her arms around her knees. "I'm not going to accept blame for that."

"Can you accept that I'm falling in love with you?"

Her head turned toward him slowly, and she looked as if she was going to jump up and run away. "Please don't say that, Noah."

"And why shouldn't I say it, Viviana?"

"Because you don't know what you're saying. You don't know me, and I certainly don't know you."

Don't miss
Dealmaker, Heartbreaker *by Rochelle Alers,*
available May 2019 wherever
Harlequin® Special Edition books and ebooks are sold.

www.Harlequin.com

Copyright © 2019 by Rochelle Alers

HSEEXP0419R

Looking for more satisfying love stories with community and family at their core?

Check out **Harlequin® Special Edition** and **Love Inspired®** books!

New books available every month!

CONNECT WITH US AT:

Facebook.com/groups/HarlequinConnection

Facebook.com/HarlequinBooks

Twitter.com/HarlequinBooks

Instagram.com/HarlequinBooks

Pinterest.com/HarlequinBooks

ReaderService.com

HARLEQUIN®

ROMANCE WHEN YOU NEED IT

HFGENRE2018